Samuel Rutherford Crockett

Dulce Cor

Being the Poems of Ford Bereton

Samuel Rutherford Crockett

Dulce Cor
Being the Poems of Ford Bereton

ISBN/EAN: 9783744772716

Printed in Europe, USA, Canada, Australia, Japan

Cover: Foto ©Andreas Hilbeck / pixelio.de

More available books at **www.hansebooks.com**

"THE LADY BEATRICE"

DULCE COR

BEING

THE POEMS OF FORD BERÊTON

" My youth 's dear book "
VITA NUOVA

LONDON
KEGAN PAUL, TRENCH & CO., 1, PATERNOSTER SQUARE
MDCCCLXXXVI

To you, *my heart's* Sweet Heart,
 Ideal still to me,
My *life's far better* part—
 To *you,* O *wife to* be,

Wherever thou *mayst wait,*
By *what dear* trysting-gate,
Thy feet all wet with dew,
 Thy youth's clear dew—

Dear Muse, so often sought,
 Tender and wise and true,
I dedicate anew
My 'youth's dear book' to you,

Howe'er imperfect wrought
Its Pansies of pure thought,
With Rosemary for remembrance,
 And Rue, sweet Rue, for you.

FOREWORD.

In the ancient Abbey of *Dulce Cor,*
The pleasant Solway near,
Two passionate hearts they laid of yore
And a love that cast out fear.

And still love casts out fear,
And hearts like the passionate hearts of yore
Throb in the Abbey of *Dulce Cor,*
The pleasant Solway near.

Sweet Heart Abbey,
1885.

"When John Baliol died in 1269 Devorgilla, his wife, had his dear heart embalmed and enshrined in a coffer of ivory, enamelled and bound with silver bright, which was placed before her daily in her hall as her sweet silent companion. At her death she desired the relic to be laid upon her heart, when sleeping in the New Abbey which she caused to be built. Hence it received the name of Sweet Heart Abbey."—*Scoti Monasticon.*

CONTENTS.

MEMORY HARVEST.

R. M. M.

I.

ANOTHER year it is! The full spring tide
  Throbs in the heart of nature and of man.
    It sweeps the drift of other years than these—
  The spoil of summer, wrack of winter wan,
    Flotsam and jetsam of all memories,
      Far up the shingly side
Of that long barrier-reef we call our Past,
    Which groweth hungrier with the ebbing years,
    Burying far down high hopes and bitter fears,
Leaving naught bare for long the seas upcast!

II.

Shall we then make our harvest of the sea
  And garner memories, which we surely deem
    May light these hearts of ours on darksome days,
  When loneliness hath power, and no kind beam
    Lightens about our feet the perilous ways?
      For of Eternity

This present hour is all we call our own,
   And Memory's edge is dull'd, even as it brings
   The sunny swathes of unforgotten springs,
And sweeps them to our feet like grass long mown.

III.

From out the dark one gloaming shineth bright, *
   When in Fate's door Love placed his golden key—
   A dull December day with spurts of hail,
And fine frost garniture on bush and tree.
    O'er a white land had raved the southern mail,
      And now through early night
The city lights flash past, and all my youth
   Stirs in my heart to greet one in the hall—
   A grey-eyed maid, as comely, sweet, and tall,
As in Judean fields the gleaner Ruth.

IV.

There is an eve in the sweet prime of **June**
   Agleam with Love's fierce light, a twilight **sky**
    Shot through with arrows of a man's **despair**—
Grey seas' monotony, low mists that lie
   Along the tideless flats, a lonely **pair**
    In that intense commune
Which blots the future and the past, which makes
   The passers-by seem idle phantom shapes ;
   Till, born in fire and dark, twin Love escapes,
And in their eyes June's sweetest morning breaks.

V.

A day of sunny showers, filled with the scent
   Of leaves, sun-smitten ere the dews were dry;
      The path, one dazzling glow of hawthorn bloom,
   And underfoot were daisies, and the shy
      Red roses beckoning from the woodland gloom;
         The graceful foxgloves bent
To cool their ladyfingers in the rills;
     Yet through the gladness in the eyes of each
     We read, that perfect joy hath power to teach
Even sadder things than plenitude of ills.

VI.

Another eve I cannot choose but name,
   Nor fail to tell of reunited hands
      Warm after severance—of eyes that scarce
   Left hold of eyes—the wonderful new lands,
      The purple plain of sea, the gentle airs
         That through the hill-gaps came—
These were the half-seen setting to our joy;
     New bliss unrealized warmed us like wine,
     And happier hearts than these of thine and mine
Had not the Master in his world-employ.

VII.

A bounteous month of joy that August was,
   Filled with low voice of seas, and lower voice
      Of love, and warm with love's intensest heart!

See where the hills dip down, hearken the noise
 Of falling waters, eager to depart
  From off the crags and pass
Into the cool green ocean depths.   The land
 Singeth aloud for love ; and crimson flush
 The skies at eve and morn ; the uplands blush
In sheets of heather blossom where we stand.

VIII.

Give me thine hand, sweet love ! it is not meet
 Thou should'st be silent when the world doth sing !
  Or is thy silence gladder than my words ?
Poor words ! and yet what sweetness shall they bring
 When this our cup of joy seems broken shards
  Lying about our feet !
" BEHOLD, I LOVE THEE !"   From the midst of this
 The fairest scene beneath the canopy,
 An echo cometh, " *Thee*," and only " *Thee !*"
O love, BE *silent—answer with a kiss!*

IX.

And ah ! the sacred morns that crowned the week—
 The path betwixt the mountains and the sea,
  The Sannox water and the wooden bridge,
 The little church, the narrow seats—and we
  That through the open window saw the ridge
   Of Fergus, and the peak

Of utmost **Cior Mohr**—nor held it wrong,
  When **vext** with platitude and stirless air,
    To watch the mist wreaths clothe the rock-scarps
      bare,
And in the pauses hear the blackbird's song.

X.

O nest, leaf-hidden, Dryad's green alcove,
  Half-islanded by hill-brook's seaward rush,
    My love's still bower, where none may come but I !
  Where in clear morning prime and high noon hush
    With only some old poet's book I lie !
      Sometimes a lonely dove
Calleth her mate, or droning honey thieves
  Weigh down the bluebell's nodding campanule ;
    And ever singeth through the twilight cool
Low voice of water and the stir of leaves.

XI.

Perfect are August's golden afternoons !
  All the rough way across the fells, a peal
    Of joy-bells ring, not heard by alien ear.
  The jealous brake and close-shut beech conceal
    The sweet bower's queen and mine, albeit I hear
      Hummed scraps of dear old tunes.
I push the boughs aside, and lo, I look
  Upon a sight to make one more than wise,—
    A true maid's heart, shining from tender eyes,
Rich with love's lore, unlearnt in any book.

XII.

Sweet is this girl as heart's-ease after rain—
   A sudden wonder to the wayfarers,
     Like silver-gleaming birch in dusk of pines !
   Ah ! Paris never saw that head of hers,
     Sun-touched in gloom of leaves as now it shines,
      Else Troy had saved her pain ;
   For head of Juno port, Minerva's eyes,
     Queen Venus' grace upon her island strand,
      Hath this dear maid—so from the shepherd's hand,
   She takes the apple with a sweet surprise.

XIII.

And if this beauty fitly doth enshrine
   A maid's pure troth, how fitly that of wife !
     O subtle essence, meaning ultimate
   Of Love's dear mystery, life's inner life !
     We feel thy power, and eagerly await
      Till thou arise and shine,
   O Sun of final union, on our bliss.
     Shine quickly—give our hearts a welcome rest,
     For loneliness is lonely at the best,
   And partner'd poverty more sweet than this !

XIV.

Through the light tresses of the birchen copse
   The sun sprays down a wealth of wavering gold ;
     And with a rustle like my lady's skirt

The winds draw close the leaves about our fold.
 Deep-bosom'd in the cool ravine, and girt
  By scorching treeless slopes,
In the deep tide of bliss our hearts we steep—
 The same sad hearts that now in silence mourn—
 Were there no hope in God, O love forlorn,
The memory of these days might make us weep !

XV.

Yet is there hope, for we in God have trust,
 And in ourselves—knowing He will not let
  Slip from His hand two lives, that He hath
   brought
 Together by strange ways—doth not forget
  To finish well the web Himself hath wrought !
   Is not the Weaver just ?
 Lo, He shall see His labour perfected ;
  No gracious promise registered above
  Will He permit to fail, nor this our Love
Will He let ravel like a knotless thread !

XVI.

So in this arbour green, my love and I
 In pleasant wise made short the afternoon.
  Half-hid in bracken at her feet I lay,
 Regretting not the glory of our June
  While mellow August in our grasp did stay
   And hardly did we sigh

That through our fingers did the sweet time glide,
   Being so rich in joy, we did not deem
   That one day we should waken from our dream
And in the isle of bliss no longer bide.

XVII.

Yet since each hour had its especial joy,
   Each eve to south or north along the shore
      We went, and saw the shallow sands
   Gleam through the pure ·green brine, and Sannox
        pour
      His ocean-tribute from the sterile lands ;
        Or gather'd woodflowers shy ;
   And in the gloaming came we singing home,
      Until we reach'd the parting of the ways,
      Where with my hand in hers a maiden says,
" *O love, to one more of our days an end hath come !* "

XVIII.

" Do I remember," say'st thou, " that still night,
   The harvest moon high overhead, we strayed
      Down the white road ; and over Brodick bay
   We saw the Holy Isle couch undismayed,
      Vast, vague, and leonine, and the array
        Of pilèd cloud-peaks bright
   Along the dim horizon of the South ? "
      Yea, I remember ; yet more clear I trace
      The dear surrender of one moon-lit face,
And, strangely clear, the smile about her mouth.

XIX.

One long, long August day the heather bent
  Under her feet ; still morning's young sunshine
    Caressed the pale gold hair, noon's pulsing fire
Made all her cheek's faint rose incarnadine ;
    Her eyes watch'd the low sun beyond Cantyre
      Fill all the fair extent
Of ample cloudland and the narrow seas
  With purple glamour, haze of shining gold,
  And the grey curtains of the night-mists fold
The islands of the nether Hebrides.

XX.

Not distant from her side through all that day,
  I wonder'd at the lithe grace of the maid,
    Her bearing high yet frank, as one well used
To the free airs that round the hill-tops played.
    A calm sweet nobleness of mien infused
      In men the wish to pay
The homage of their best, ever to show
  Their highest to her eyes, being so pure
  That naught unsightly can her look endure,
But, shamefaced, from her presence forth doth go.

XXI.

Just on the edge of the high table-land
  Where lies the lake, deep girdled with morass,
    We found two streams, a torrent and a brook.

Slow-winding to the verge the brook did pass,
  Over its pools heather and harebell shook,
    And brown bent stretch'd a hand
To the tall rushes on the hither side.
  Adown the mountain like a lightning flash
  From the sheer cliffs the torrent waters dash,
With the sweet valley streamlet fain to bide ;

XXII.

But from the granite basin where they meet,
  Lo, the still brook doth take the headlong pace
    And fiercer heart-throb of the mountain-born !
Through the long pass it foams in arrowy race,
  Forgetful of the still land left forlorn ;
    Behind their ardent feet
The old course lies, a scarce remember'd thread,
  As, glad at heart, they seek the parent sea—
  So of two lives this is the mystery,
And *thou* already hast the riddle read.

XXIII.

From lone October's melancholy days .
  My heart goes back, remembering all the joy
    That August held, and sweet September's bliss,
More fully known and charged with less alloy ;
    Yea, backward looking, sure I am of this,
      That love in woodland ways

Is not more sweet than by the fireside ;
　And nearest to my heart of hearts doth stay
　　The gracious duty fitly done each day,
Thy work at morn and song at eventide.

XXIV.

For wafts of unforgotten music come
　All unawares into my lonely room,
　　To thrill me with the memories of the past—
Sometimes a tender voice from out the gloom,
　A light hand on the keys, a shadow cast
　　Upon a learnèd tome
That blurs somewhat Alpha and Omega,
　A touch upon my shoulder, a pale face
　Upon whose perfect curves the fire-light plays,
Or love-lit eyes, the sweetest e'er I saw.

XXV.

These are but idle visions that I trace,
　And yet their summer radiance lights my soul.
　They tell me that this wind weeps not the loss
Of Love's ripe grain, that though the waters roll
　Firm stands our bridge of faith—it spans across
　　This empty interspace—
Its further arch springs from a land of peace
　That lieth towards the morning ; in that land
　A home for thee and me doth surely stand,
Around whose hearth-fire shall our souls find ease.

XXVI.

Far in the deep of Arden wood it lies ;
   About it pleasant leaves for ever wave.
      Through charmèd afternoons we wander on,
   And at the sundown reach the seas that lave
      The golden isles of blessed Avalon.
         When the sweet daylight dies,
   Out of the gloom the ferryman doth glide
      To take us both into a younger day ;
      And as the twilight land recedes away,
My· lady draweth closer to my side.

XXVII.

Thus to a granary for our winter need
   We bring these gleanings from the harvest field ;
      Not the full crop we bring, but only sheaves
   At random ta'en from autumn's golden yield—
      One handful from a forest's fallen leaves ;
         Yet shall this grain be seed
   Wherewith to sow the furrows year by year —
      These wither'd leaves of other springs the pledge,
      When *thou* shalt hear over our hawthorn hedge
The mavis to his own mate calling clear.

XXVIII.

For us no early sun shall ever shine,
   And never in the dusk a moon shall rise,
      But through our hearts shall run a sudden thrill

And dews of memory dim the yearning eyes.
 The clouds that cast their shadows on the hill,
  The mist's swift changing line,
Upon the sea the sheets of driving rain—
 These are, and pass, like to a tale well told ;
 But Life and Love shall not so slip our hold,
While suns and moons like these with us remain.

1883.

FORD BERÊTON.

I.

THREADING through the ripening barley,
Up the long rigs of the corn,
'Cross the meadows, with their mallows
Wet with dews of early morn,
Through the waving oats and barley,
With his friend, four-footed Charley,
Ford Berêton sought the shallows,
Where the swift white-breasted swallows
Dash and flash above the river.

Taller just a single handbreadth
On his sun-burnt flitting feet
Than the creamy meadow-sweet—
He, the sweetheart of the meadows,
Of the trembling woodland shadows,
Of the flowers and of the hours,
Sweetheart of the wood-folk hidden
In the dim wych-hazel bowers !
River-fairies kiss'd unbidden

His red mouth as he lay dreaming,
With his hair's gold auriole gleaming
　As the sun peep'd in to see.
Bright as early sunshine he,
Well-beloved, well beloving,
As the winds and waters free ;
All alone, but unforsaken,
Hush'd was Ford by summer bees,
Watch'd by bright-eyed irises ;

　And in meadows, half-awaken
Heard he chimes of harebells, shaken
Merrily by small flower-angels.

　All the day these glad evangels
Rang like music in his ear,
Woodland words and mysteries
Of the flowery lakeland leas.

　Though his heart rang clear and true
To the human love he knew,
Still to them his heart was truer,
To the sunshine and the trees—
Wooed them like an ardent wooer　　.
All the morning of his life ;
For the summer sun was clearer,
And the August wind was dearer,
Circling round the fields at strife,
Rustling strife, and whispering parley
With the hosts of armed barley,
In the wide fields by the lake.

Hardly dearer was the human
Love of tender loving woman,
Quiet eyes and sad caresses,
Than the upland winds' embraces,
   And the song of woodland bird.

Ford's small heart was not untender ;
But as yet it had not stirr'd
In response to love unwearied,
Nor could see the soft brown tresses
Fading into softer grey.

   Instant was he to defend her
Fiercely with small fist and tongue,
Like a wild-cat brought to bay,
Desperate to guard its young ;
Yet he broke from her still keeping,
Eager for the moorlands ever,
For the heather and the river,
And the summer sunshine steeping
Lake and hill and yellow corn.
Much he griev'd her mother's mildness
With his wandering and his wildness.
Then when bitter bread of grudging
Or the ache of unthank'd drudging,
Pain'd in her sore heart the sorest—
Lost was Ford within the forest,
Lost with Charley, Tweed, or Royal,
Good dogs all, and champions loyal,
Since the earliest break of morn.

Then at evening, scratch'd and torn
On the hawthorn hedges jagged,
Wonder small that clothes were ragged—
Wonder small that one was bending
Carefully above her mending
Half the night with fingers worn;
While within his crib unwinking,
Ford slept sound and dreamless sleep.

In the morning, never thinking
How his clothes were once more mended,
Folded in well-order'd heap,
Ford would dress, and to the sheep
And his shepherd friend would run.
Just as apt was Ford at races
With his flocks of horn'd black faces,
As his friends with twice as many
Feet to twinkle in the sun.
True it was, Ford had not any
Tail to wave aloft in air;
But a sturdy right arm had he,
By the elder people's showing
Over apt at pebble-throwing.

Yet did Ford his honest share
Of the shouting and hallooing,
Of the turning and pursuing,
And of all that was adoing
At the folding and unfolding,

At the washing and the smearing,
And the great day of the shearing—
Hounding on or backward holding,
Up and down, and to and fro,
Mad with rapture, Ford would go !

II.

But on this especial morn
Ford went onward through the corn,
Past the warren and the sunny
Haunts of crop-ear'd, white-tail'd bunny,
To his den far out of reach—
Overhung by sweet-leaf'd beech,
Underwash'd by limpid water,
Just above the great black pool
Where last year Ford saw the otter.

Here in hidden cave enchanted,
Was the spot by Ford most haunted ;
Safe and secret, still and cool,
For, by whomsoever wanted,
Here was rest from alien rule.

Ford could see the fishes swimming,
Not a stain the water dimming ;
Rippling crisply o'er the stones—
Silent, save for undertones
From the hazel copse behind,
Fretted by the fitful wind,
And the shallow river bickering

O'er the sloping, pebbly reaches—
Dusky, yet with sunshine flickering
Through the leaves on either hand
On the tiny silver beaches,
  And the shining granite sand.

On his throne, moss overgrown,
King Berêton sits him down ;
Looks upon his kingdom narrow,
Lays aside his bow and arrow,
Calls his subjects to his presence !
  Forth with ready acquiescence
Two mice come and one lame sparrow.
  Lastly ruddy Robin Redbreast,
Who with smooth and plumply fed breast,
Sits a-swing upon the pliant
Hazel-branches, nearer comes
For his hoarded dole of crumbs
  Like a gentlemanly client.

Unto them doth Boy Berêton,
Leaning back his mossy seat on,
Slow propound his latest query.

Stiffly propp'd upon the arrow
Stood His Majesty's own sparrow, .
All-important, wise, and cheery ;
Also, having finish'd eating,
Both the field-mice back retreating,

Curious peer'd from out their hole.
 Ford laid down his broad blue bonnet,
Red-breast calmly took his dole,
Wiped his beak, and stepp'd upon it.
 Courtier he, but no King's minion,
Not averse to give opinion
And consider critically
 Even the King's philosophy.

1884.

FORD BERÊTON.

" Do you know the silver birches,
Just below the hawthorn hedges,
On the great black forest's edges ? "
    For reply, Sir Robin perches
On the bonnet's woollen tassel,
Bows like an obedient vassal,
    Till the King is satisfied
With his subject's strict attention.
" Then I hardly need to mention
Whom I saw so quickly hide,
In the leaves of that wild cherry,
In his beak a big fat berry
Stolen from our orchard croft ! "

    Here His Highness frown'd severely,
And Sir Robin calmly coughed,
Just to show how very clearly
This was no affair of his.

" In the field so wide and sunny
Where the summer clover is,
Where each year the mower searches
For the nests of wild-bee honey,
All along these silver birches
Stand up straight in shining row,
Dewdrops sparkling, shadows darkling,
In the early morning glow ;
And in gloaming time they're gleaming
White, like angels when I'm dreaming.

" There among its handsome brothers
Was one little crooked tree,
Different from all the others,
Just as bent as bent could be.
   First it crawl'd along the heather
Till it turn'd up straight again,
Then it drew itself together
Like a tender thing in pain ;
Scarce a single green leaf straggled
From its twigs so bare and draggled—
And it really looks asham'd
When I'm passing by that way,
Just as if it tried to say—
   ' Please don't look at such a maim'd
Little Cripple-Dick as I ;
Look at all the rest about,
Look at them and pass me by,

I'm so crooked, do not flout me,
  Kindly turn your head awry ;
Of what use is my poor gnarl'd
Body in this lovely world ? '

" Then I cried for very sorrow,
And I went up close to say,
  ' I must run now, but to-morrow
    I shall bring my dog and stay ;
  We'll not sit below the great ones
    Though they are so very tall,
  Nor below the leafiest straight ones,
    For I love you best of all.'
Then around its little twisted
Crippl'd waist I put my arm,
Drew it close to me and kiss'd it
Where the sunshine makes it warm.

" *Robin Red-breast, are you listening ?* "
Like a knight upon his castle,
Or a captain on the poop,
Robin with his bright eyes glistening
Stood upon the bonnet's tassel,
Head aside and wings a-droop.

" So that day I ask'd at dinner,
' Can a birch-tree be a sinner,
Or grow twisted out and in
For some elder birch's sin ? '

So they said, ' Depend upon it,
Here's some new bee in his bonnet ! '
But I had no bee at all—
Only sprigs of meadow-gall.

" In the afternoon again,
I did ask my uncle Ben,
   ' When at first God made the creatures
And the garden trees for food,
Didn't he look on all their features
And pronounce them very good?
Can a God of such good will,
Make lame birches on the hill?'
   ' Go,' he said, ' go carry water—
Fit you better than to chatter
What you cannot understand !'

" And I think he would have beat me,
But that Royal from the sheep
Just then bounded up to greet me,
Growling in his throat so deep,
That he quickly went to stand
T'other side the garden paling.

" So I asked as he was nailing
Weasels to the orchard wall—
   ' All things that are very wicked
Does God make them crook'd and small?'
' No,' he answered, ' little thick-head ;
Pests and weeds wax best of all !' "

What the sense of that might be
Ford Berêton could not see.

Solemnly these questions deep
To the sparrow he propounded ;
But as he was much confounded,
Having early gone to sleep,
And the field-mice long had rested
  Cosily within their den,
Prompt solution he requested
  From Sir Robin Red-breast then—
Down stepp'd he and peck'd a crumb,
For the rest, was wisely dumb.

So, when Ford went on the morrow,
Lo, he found with bitter sorrow,
From the roots his birch uptorn,
Saw it cross the meadow borne,
Watch'd in pleasant wood-shed, scented
With the chips of fresh-cut pine,
As his grand-sire carv'd and bent it
  To a rustic quaint design,
Made a chair with arms well curv'd
  And a back well-smooth'd and fine.

" Thine, my boy, and well-deserv'd
By that tender heart of thine,
For from straightest trees," he said,
" Seats like this are never made ;

But for small and crooked birches
Carefully the woodman searches."
Kindly thus Ford's old grandfather,
" Do not weep, my lad, but rather
Joy that God can bring from weakness,
    Service noble, fit, and long :
And may thou and I in meekness
    Be built up as firm and strong.
Every crooked thing that grows
Hath a use the Master knows ! "

So, his well-beloved seat on
Nightly sitteth Boy Berêton.

1885.

FORD BERÊTON.

HIS WONDERING.

IN the long grass of the meadow
Ford Berêton sits and talketh,
To his small self in the shadow.
With his wooden sword he knocketh
Somewhat fiercely on the capping
Of his iron-girded foot gear.
Problems strange hath Ford Berêton,
So his own folks call him "queer."
Argument of knuckle rapping
Mostly solves the awkward question,

" Can your elders never learn you,"
Oft they argued in this fashion,
"To leave what does not concern you
With much wiser heads than yours? "

Once a master, quick in passion,
Closed discussion with a blow ;

Unto whom straightway Berêton :
"'Hold your hand, sir,' does not answer
Little boys who want to know."

To this furious dominie
Dauntlessly quoth Boy Berêton.

" Now, I wonder "
(This was ever Ford's beginning)
" If I'm really always sinning
Like the grown folk say I am ?
Uncle Ben says last night's thunder
Was God's anger sent to frighten
Wicked little boys who lifted
The great sluices of the dam,
Just to hear the mill-wheel splashing,
Just to see the sunlight sifted
Through the drops as they come flashing
From the big brown wooden boxes
Down the mill-race to the pool.
Now, I don't think God unlocks His
Thunder chamber in the heaven,
And makes all the black sky lighten
Just to scare one little boy,
Who is hardly yet turned seven !"

(Ford thought God would not employ
So much cry for little wool.
This was childish, I confess ;

But you know the lad was small.
So I pray, wise people all,
Pardon him this foolishness.)

" Now, I wonder "—Ford a moment
Sideways poised his head to listen,
A far voice that called his name,
Then resumed without a comment.
" Now, I wonder,"—pause to squeeze
Clover tops between his palms,
Sucking honey like the bees—
" What a living Pharisee is?
There's my uncle Ben, now he is
Just that kind who sneak and bother,
Never helping blind or lame,
Like those who follow'd Christ.

" Preachman came one day to sing,
Asked severely, ' *Ford, who made you?* '
' God,' I said, ' made everything.'
Wasn't he stupid not to know?
Turn about, I asked another,
' *Did the God also make you?* '
Easier one couldn't ask,
Yet they took me so to task,
Just for saying when he nodded,
' Is that true?   Well, then, if God did,
I am sure He must have weigh'd you
On His biggest pair of scales!'

Why they put me out, and made me
Carry water from the spring—
More than twenty pair of pails—
I could not think.   Maybe my feet
Made the new carpet dirty, or
They wanted just to shut the door.
Christ would not shut the door, I know,
Nor call me off that shining street
Where the fair white angels sing."

Reader, prithee kindly pardon
Ford his foolish childish notions ;
Far from church, among the moors,
Dwelt the lad.   Friends, be not hard on
Childish words not wise like yours.
Ford to church but once had been
Where he much disturbed devotions,
With the injudicious queries,
" Why must Fordie shut his eyes ? "
" Will that man not soon be done ? "

" Now I'm sure "—the preface varies,
" If I held Christ by the hand,
And I asked for all I'm wanting
So to know, He wouldn't say,
' You're too young to understand ;
Now, don't bother, go away ! '
Now I wonder, when they christened

Me, O *such* a time ago "
(Here again he paused and listened
Very near he heard his name),
Maybe they forgot to make me
Good, like story-boys, you know !
And I wonder, if the Christ came,
Would He send me out or take me
In our parlour on His knee,
As He used to do those other
Little lads in Galilee ?
Now I have not any brother ;
If I had, I'd ask Christ Jesus,
And He'd take him up and hold him,
Like He lov'd him, tenderly—
Then I'd climb the other knee ! "

Suddenly is closed the thesis,
Nemesis his collar seizes,
Roughly setteth Ford his feet on ;
Endeth quest of Boy Berêton.

1884.

FORD BERETON.

HIS HOME COMING.

" And it shall come to pass that I will put thee in a clift of the
rock, and will cover thee with my hand while I pass by."

CRISPLY up the frozen road,
Roaming here and there abroad,
Ford Berêton's small feet clatter'd ;
Starting rabbits out of hedges,
Waterfowl from fenny sedges,
Hares along the pasture's edges,
    Scapegrace dog and master strode.

Weightier-footed than his master,
In the twilight Royal patter'd
O'er the stiff grass grey with frost,
Swinging slow or bounding faster
    Like a stalwart canine ghost.

See, they cross the fertile fallows,
Now the ice-bound lake-side shallows ;
Soon they enter on the poor lands
Of the burnt and matted heather,
Waste morass and trackless moorlands,
　　Ranging heedlessly together.

What reck they of black horizon,
Or of inky gloom that lies on
All the bleak blue mountain ranges,
As the face of nature changes,
And the landmarks dimmer grow
　　With the coming of the snow.

First the broad far-sailing flakes
Fall in silence slow and heavy ;
Then a mirthful dancing bevy
Scuds across the sullen lakelets.
Soon a moaning wind awaking
All the heavy cloud-folds shaking,
Drives the steady stinging flakelets,
Making Ford's cheeks redder glow
　　In the turmoil of the snow.

How the pair rejoiced and revelled,
Leapt and barked and laughed and shouted,
Charged abreast and fell back routed,
Clenched and fought and rolled dishevelled
　　In the snow-drifts to and fro !

D

"Find the way now, good dog Royal!"
Struggling upward quoth the boy, all
Sober'd with the ghastly starkness
Of the single spectral birches
In the swiftly growing darkness;
"Seek it, seek it out, good Royal!"
And the great dog, strong and loyal,
Through the snow-wreaths round and round
All about the moorland searches,
With his nose against the ground,
Sought and sought and never found.

In the silence yet more dreary
Boy Berêton's limbs grew weary,
Courage waned with Royal gone;
Wearier grew they till he rested,
Chill and heartless, on a stone
In a covert grim and eery
    Deep among the sheltering rocks.

From the pocket on his side
Slow he drew the precious box,
Where his mice had lived together
    In their cave of finest wool.
Scarce a week ago one died,
Frost-nipp'd by the icy weather,
And was borne in funeral
From the threshold of the school

To its grave beneath the wall,
With the pomp of mourners all.

As he opens, beaded eyes
O'er the edge a moment rise.
One small hand the mouse doth hold,
With the other, blue and cold,
On its smooth head he caressed it ;
For a space forgetful smiled
At the outer darkness wild,
Smiled to see it crouch and nestle
In its cosy bed of wool ;
In his bosom heard it rustle,
As he stamped his frozen feet on
Narrow ledge not yet invaded
    By the fast encroaching snows.

Instantly the gladness faded
As the drifting snow came sweeping,
Heavy wreaths in silence heaping
Sheltered nook and stony seat on.
" Well, at least," quoth Boy Berêton,
" Mousie's warm, though I am cold ! "

" Now I wonder," with a flicker
Of the old Ford in his eyes
As he watched the snow come thicker,
" Are the angels warm and rosy
When the snow-storms fill the skies,

As in summer when the sun
Makes their cloud-beds warm and cosy?
And I wonder if they're sleeping
Through this bitter winter weather;
Or aloft their watches keeping,
As the shepherds said of them,
Hosts and hosts of them together,
Singing o'er the lowly stable,
  In that little Bethlehem!"

And the pitying angels slowly
Sang their Christ songs, pure and holy,
As they saw his limbs grow rigid
And his features blue and frigid;
And God hearkened more his wonderings
Than the starry chariots' thunderings—
  Shoutings of the sons of God.

Ford's young feet had never trod
In the devious way that brings
Doubts and fatal questionings.
Early trusted he the sorrow
Wrought on Israel's Calvary,
Trusted God for each to-morrow,
Asking not what God might be.

" Wonder who will come and take me
From the snow, so white and deep?
If it's very hard to die,

Or like going fast asleep,
Only just a little sounder ?
Maybe Christ Himself will wake me,
Maybe let His Mary-mother
Comfort mine, and throw around her
   Arms that nursed Him when a boy.

" And however bad am I,
He would let me be His lamb,
Rather than with Lazarus lie
On the breast of Abraham !

" Maybe God sends him the grown ones,
While the little lambs, the lone ones,
Go to the Lord Jesus' bosom.
And I wonder if my mousie
Will be sleeping in his housie
   When they find me in the snow ? "

Here grew Ford a little drowsy,
Looked one way and then another,
Only saw the snow keep falling,
All his tiny covert walling
   From the world of warmth and home.

Feebly now the slow words come,
" Good night, mousie ; good night, mother :
Take me, Christ, to Thee to keep—
I'll be warmer when I waken.
Coming, mother—I am coming."

But 'twas Death, with fingers numbing,
Through the darkness that was coming
  In the sheeted silence deep.

Distant murmurs, rising, falling,
Barking dogs and shepherds calling :
Great red Royal, far before,
Finds the body of his master,
And like one who fears disaster,
To the heavens calling " Faster,"
Sends a great deep-throated roar ;
And the shepherds round and round
Shake the welkin, echoing, " FOUND ! "

And at home when they undress'd him,
Lo, one frozen hand firm closing
Round the cage deep in his breast—
Inside, mousie warmly dozing !

This the tender little mother,
Bending over to caress him,
Joying in each soft drawn breath,
Heard in silence still as death,
Trying hard her sobs to smother,
With her face against the wall—
" Mother, mother, please don't wake me ;
Dear Lord Christ has come to take me—
  Me and mousie, cage and all ! "

1885.

A LEAF FROM THE DAMASK ROSE.

THERE'S a leaf in the book of the damask rose
    That glows with a tender red ;
From the bud through the bloom to the dust it goes,
    Into rose dust fragrant and dead.

And this word is inscribed on the petals fine
    Of that velvety purple page—
" Be true to thy youth while yet it is thine
    Ere it sink in the mist of age,

>   *" Ere the bursting bud be grown*
>   *To a rose nigh overblown,*
>   *And the wind of the autumn eves*   ·
>   *Comes blowing and scattering all*
> *The damask drift of the dead rose leaves*
> *Under the orchard wall.*

" Like late-blown roses the joy-days flit,
    And soon will the east winds blow ;
  So the love years now must be lived and writ
    In red on a page of snow.

" And here the rune of the rose I rede,
    'Tis the heart of the rose and me—
O youth, O maid, in your hour of need,
    Be true to the sacred three—
Be true to the love that is love indeed,
    To thyself, and thy God, these three !

> " *Ere the bursting bud is grown*
> *To a rose nigh overblown,*
> *And the wind of the autumn eves*
> *Comes blowing and scattering all*
> *The damask drift of the dead rose leaves*
> *Under the orchard wall.*"

1885.

THE BELLS OF ANTWERP.

I.

WHAT of the night, O Antwerp bells,
 Over the city swinging,
Plaintive and sad, O kingly bells,
 In the winter midnight ringing ?

And the winds in the belfry moan
From the sand-dunes waste and lone,
 And these are the words they say,
 The turreted bells and they—

" *Callerhout, Krabbendyk,* **Calloo,**"
 Say the noisy, turbulent crew ;
"*Jabbeké,* **Chaam, Waterloo ;**
Hoggerhaed, Sandvaet, **Lilloo,**
We are weary, a-weary **of you !**
We sigh for the hills of snow,
For the hills where the hunters go,
For the Matterhorn, Wetterhorn, Dom,
 For the Dom ! *Dom !* *Dom !*

For the summer sun and the rustling corn,
And the pleasant vales of the Rhineland valley."

II.

What of the morn, O Antwerp bells ?
In the east is the daybreak shining ?
Hasten your chimes by an hour, O bells ;
Peace, O winds, from your pestilent whining—

" *Callerhout, Krabbendyk, Calloo,"*
Go the jangling, turbulent crew ;
"*Jabbeké, Chaam, Waterloo,*
Hoggerhaed, Sandvaet, Lilloo,
We are weary, a-weary of you !"

And the wind complain'd as it went on its way,
And this was its plaintive lay—
" *Ischia, Spezzia, Bex,*
Isola Bella, and Aix,
To be aye and aye and aye,
In the summer sun; and the rustling corn,
And the pleasant vales of the Rhineland valley."

III.

What of the day, O Antwerp bells?
Silvery clear your warning,
·For the wailing winds had gone on their way,
Ere ye rang your chimes in the morning.

Never more, never more they say,
  " *Callerhout, Krabbendyk, Calloo,*"
    That jangling, turbulent crew,
  "*Jabbeké, Chaam, Waterloo,*
  Hoggerhaed, Sandvaet, Lilloo,
    We are weary, a-weary of you."

They were weary of Bergen-op-Zoom,
  Of a land as dull as the tomb,
Of the boisterous bells of Boom,
  With their **Boom,** *Boom, Boom,*
    And black-a-vised *Hollander gloom.*

They have gone where the birds all sing,
Where the ring doves mate in the spring ;
    And what say ye to-day
    Ere I too go on my way—
  From your belfry carv'd and grey ?

  " *Canterbury, Winchester, Bray,*
    Edinburgh, Elderslie, Spey—
O the summer sun and the rustling **corn,**
And pleasanter vales than the Rhineland valley."

A SUMMER DAY.

AWAY from the city's blistering heat,
From clang of crank and piston's beat,
We stray'd down Chester's galleried street
   To the bank of her dreaming river.

For not her glamour **of** grey renown,
Nor minster turrets shining down
On the broad-walled old cathedral **town,**
   Might hold **us long from the river.**

Sweet was the shade in the cloisters dim,
Sweet the choir-boys' chanted hymn ;
But sweeter the wind on the water's rim
   And the iris beds in the river.

   Ripple of water, drip of oar,
   Hum of bee on the blossom'd shore,
   Stirr'd not the silence the landscape wore,
      A summer day long on the river.

In still procession pass they by
The hidden blooms in the coves that **lie**,
And the trees that underarch the sky
   And shadow the dreaming river.

Sweetest of all, from her cushion'd ease,
A girl's eyes watch'd the daisied leas,
And shy little ringlets played with **the** breeze
   That played with the dreaming river.

   Ripple of water, drip of oar,
   Hum of bee on the blossom'd shore;
   *But sweeter than aught that the May **wind bore***
     Was my love's low voice on the river.

O love, true love, with the eyes so grey,
What love more meet for a summer's day,
For a breathless afternoon in **May**,
   On the breast of an English river.

And yet there comes as I gaze on thee,
Of bitterest storms the memory,
Of surging waves on a winter sea
   Far out from a summer river.

Of a ship hard press'd on a wild grey main,
Swept by the spray and the thunder rain,
Of two that hardly hoped again
   To float on a summer river.

Of a white girl hand that was strong alway,
Two brave and faithful eyes of grey,
And a love as meet for wintriest day
　　As for summer's noon on the river.

Therefore I hold thee, love of mine,
Precious above the gold most fine,
Far more fair than the white sunshine
　　That is bathing this summer river.

　Ripple of water, drip of oar,
　Hum of bee on *the blossom'd shore,*
　Sing in my *heart, though I no more*
　　Float with my *love on the* **river.**

1884.

ALONE.

WHAT wilt thou leave me, O belovèd,
   But the trees and the hollow skies?
Wilt thou take from me the life of life,
   And the glory of thine eyes?

Did we not watch the sun together,
   Thou in the stillness, I by thee?
Did I watch the sunset or thee, my sweet?
   Thine eyes, or the far-hung sea?

A lily ensheathed art thou, O love,
   In the hues of the folded rose,
Fresher than earliest summer flower
   To her matins as she goes.

I see my love in the sullen night
   With a glory around her hair;
And the night is darker all about
   Because that her face is fair.

In the beeches above I hear the wind,
From the south a message bring ;
Is the willow-whisper the sob of her voice,
Or the birch trees' murmuring ?

For my love hath a voice most tender-sweet,
With a thrill of pain in its tone,
Like the throbbing strings of the pine-wood harp
When the winds therein make moan.

But the barrèd doors shall fall apart,
And her voice from silence break—
The gladsome strength of jubilant morn
In the heart of midnight wake.

1883.

NOT ALONE.

On a morn when the seas are flashing blue,
  And the hills stand round about,
From the lintels low of a seaward door
  Is not this my love looks out,

With a morning sweetness deep in her eyes,
  And a lithe grace as she goes?
Wilt thou come, my love, up the sides of the glen?
  I will find thee a sweet wild rose.

The heights of the hills above our heads
  In a glamour of glory lie,
As we pass hand-joined as lovers should
  'Twixt the speedwell and the sky.   '

Clasped are our hearts as hand holds hand,
  Strength-stayed for the rockiest road ;
Not the thinnest veil keeps our spirits twain,
  And nothing keeps us from God.

1883.

THE CHOICE OF HERAKLES.

PLEASURE.　　　　HERAKLES.　　　　VIRTUE.

PLEASURE.

COME, Herakles, and I will show to thee
The places where the hidden treasures be—
The riches and the joy of life.　Come now
And pluck the ruddy apple from the bough ;
Take thou thy joy on flowery beds of ease,
Deep in the orchards of the Hesperides.

VIRTUE.

Nay, Herakles, be wise as thou art strong,
And go thou through the kingdoms righting wrong ;
For the springtime is now upon the earth,
When every husband sows his garden garth.
This is thy seedtime too, O Herakles ;
Be heedful, therefore, of thy destinies.
The stern-browed Fates no second choice allow ;
If thou would'st reap, drive straight thy furrow now.

PLEASURE.

But see, I pray, where each glad Bacchanal
Lieth at length beneath the vine-clad wall.
The languid lutes plead through the enchanted air
To banish far dull thought and barren care ;
And tendance sweet of snowy-bosomed maid
Shall Aphrodite send thee in the shade.
Yea, peradventure thou herself may'st meet,
The dewdrops kissing both her dainty feet.

HERAKLES.

Take me, O fair one, to thy land of bliss,
My lips are parch'd for Aphrodite's kiss.

VIRTUE.

Abide thee, **Herakles**; consider well
Among what folk thou dost desire to dwell ;
For Zeus himself may not his life recast,
Nor change one jot the unreturning Past.
Albeit thou shalt not couch on asphodel,
Neither shall fair-hair'd Circe cast her spell,
Nor o'er the golden chalice subtly smile,
In the high palace of her woodland isle ;
Work shalt thou have, one maiden for thy wife,
And honour from good women all thy life.
Come, Herakles, and Hebe shall rejoice,
And forth shall ring Selene's silver voice ;

With godlike kisses twain shall greet thee there,
Grey-eyed Athene, red-lipped Demeter.

PLEASURE.

Ah, thou and I are human, Herakles ;
We do not love to herd with deities,
Nor sit at the Olympian council-board ;
But Laughter shall we have for bosom-lord,
And Dionysian mysteries shall see
In the sweet glades of sacred Thessaly.
 Lo, in the dance the wine-drench'd coronal
From shoulder white and golden hair doth fall !
Anigh his breast each youth doth hold a head,
Twin flushing cheeks, and locks unfilleted,
Swifter and swifter doth the revel move
Athwart the dim recesses of the grove.
 Come, then, and all these things thou **shalt assay,**
O mighty son of Zeus and Alkmene.

VIRTUE.

O Herakles, **and wast thou** made for this,
These thews and sinews for unworthy bliss ?
Thy godlike limbs to grace a Maenad's dance,
For any wanton's kiss that countenance ?
But thou, if amaranth thou make thy bed,
Shalt never see thy labours perfected,
Nor gain the meed of all the people's praise,
Nor win Olympus after many days.

Deeds great and mighty wait for thee to do,
A world of perilous quests to venture through,
To save the folk of many an ancient state
From beast that lays their borders desolate ;
And Earth-Preserver shall thy name be called ;
On thy stout shoulders thou the world shalt hold ;
Thine oaken club shall be a name of fear,
And in thine hand the ashen-shafted spear.
A god-like sacrifice they shall thee bring,
Yea, many a crisp-wooled ram for offering ;
And in thy need Pallas Athene grave
From Erebos and Hades shall thee save.

HERAKLES.

O white-robed maid, no craven heart am I,
Nor fear the press where arrows hurtling fly,
And through the shield crashes the driven spear—
On dreadful days thou shalt the war-cry hear—
" Aoi, Herakles, son of Zeuspatér ! "
    And yet, O Queen, why should one shun to care
In his hot youth for youthful dalliance ?
Do not the young lambs in the meadows dance
From mere delight to live ?   Then why not we,
The young blood in us surging like the sea ?

VIRTUE.

Art thou no better than the beast that hies
Unto the altar garlandèd and dies ?

Thou dost not so propose to spend thy life,
Till at thy throat doth grate the slayer's knife ;
If ill deeds thou wouldst shun in after time,
Do noble things in this thy youthful prime.
If to these guileful words thou giv'st no ear,
That other siren song thou need'st not fear ;
Nor shall their subtlest singing make thee yield,
Or leave thy good ship for their flowery field.
So to thine haven thou shalt win aright,
Nor leave thy bones in cold sea-caves of night,
And walk thyself, a shade 'mong shadows grey,
Through the dim realm of dread Persephone.

PLEASURE.

See, Herakles, the palace portals bright
In Cyprus burnishèd for thy delight,
Where Aphrodite reigneth in her prime,
And laughter ringeth all the summer time.
There no laborious years thou shalt endure,
Unto no tyrant king pay forfeiture,
Nor wade to Death through never-ending pain ;
There hemlock branches make a languorous gloom,
And heavy-headed poppies drip perfume
In secret arbours set in garden close ;
And all the air, one glorious breath of rose,
Shakes not a dainty petal from the trees,
Nor stirs a ripple on the Cyprian seas,—
There shalt thou quaff, in silence half-divine,

From golden cup the honey-hearted wine.
In all that land is heard no sound of pain,
Save Cytherea's doves their love complain ;
And lightfoot Dryades shall grant thy prayer,
Upon thy shoulders place their fingers fair,
And looking up, the shy love in their eyes,
Shall stir thy sluggish pulse in wondrous wise.
Waste not thy time in idly counting cost,
Or manifold delight thy soul hath lost ;
If thou deny to Love thy summer day,
What maid shall love thee in thy winter grey?

Virtue.

O son of Zeus, beware her subtle words,
Two-edged are they, and keen like battle-swords ;
For if thou yield to her thy destiny,
Close-pent in Circe's swine-stye thou shalt lie ;
Nor shalt thou 'scape by any cunning art
Till thou hast lost all thine immortal part,
And diest, as the swine do, utterly.
But trust, O Herakles, thy youth to me,
And thou shalt be immortal as thy sire.
Thou shalt attain the heart of thy desire—
The purest maid Olympus doth uphold,
Whose smile gives youth and beauty to the old—
Hebe shall love thee, Here's fairest child,
Who in the midst of heaven walks undefiled.

HERAKLES.

O maid, take thou my hand, and let us go—
Thy bondman I, in years of weal and woe !
Yea, though the way be rough and wondrous hard,
And Hades' horrid portals triply barred,
Yet with the help of gods I will pass through,
And whatsoe'er a mortal can, will do.
So help me thou, and mine own father Zeus ;
If in my veins there flows no earthly juice,
But ichor of the gods, of nectar bred,
And with ambrosial strength divinely fed—
Then shall I do great deeds undone before,
Shall win at last the high Olympian floor,
And stand the peer of god and goddess there
With Hebe at the side of Zeuspatér.

1884.

AS IN THE DAYS OF OLD.

I.

1.

QUEENLIKE along the garden path—
Stately, albeit with mien that hath
A daintier grace than daffodil,
Wind sway'd beneath a southland hill—
Cometh my queen of girls. She seems
That very maiden won in dreams,
Whose yearning eyes evanishing,
Haunted my fancy all the spring.

2.

Gruff March, thou month of storm and fret
Bring forth thine earliest violet,
Primrose, or pale anemone,
And all thy lion front make gay
With glow of gorse-bloom, flaming high
On breezy uplands near the sky ;
For at thy lamblike out-going
Was born the flower of all the spring.

3.

Say, sweet, if I could take thy hand,
And in some haunted woodland stand
With love that sanctifieth all,
Could not this love of ours recall,
In form more fair than mortal mould,
The lovers of the days of old—
Their pale sweet brows engarlanding
With the fresh flowers of this new spring?

4.

Love-passionate from depth of shade,
Would come that Galilean maid
Whom Queen's apparel never won,
Nor treasures of King Solomon ;
Ruth too, whom farmer Boaz saw,
Among the sheaves in Ephratah ;
And through the boskage, moving tall,
Sweet Eve, the mother of us all.

5.

And March himself would curb his play,
And breathe like an Arcadian May,
While in the woodlands hand in hand,
A pair of living lovers stand,
And favour'd converse gladly hold
With lovers of the days of old ;
While all the riches of the spring
Break forth in wondrous blossoming.

II.

I.

I never saw that wood save in a dream—
Nor any wight with unanointed eyes
May see the marvel—wade the flowery aisles,
Arch'd with a dim magnificence of leaves ;
Not such as Dante saw, but carpeted
With a fair carpet of the flowers of old,
Whose names I scarce can guess—not common
    blooms,
But lotus, amaranth and asphodel,
And great white lilies floating on the meres,
Fit barges for the court of Faërie.
And a blue sky o'erarch'd the forest arch,
And a blue sea enisled ; and yet the wood
Was English, and fresh English air
Puls'd in its noonday quiet.
                    I and she
Were all alone, and overhead the doves
Set all the wood a-murmuring with love ;
But other sound was none, only ourselves,
Two dreamers in a paradise of dreams.
Thus hand in hand beneath a bank of bloom
We stood, nor were afraid at all, and up
Through the sweet dim arcades a woman came,
Knit in the fashion of a larger time,
And stamp'd more clearly with the image of God ;

Who took my maid by the right hand, and look'd
Within her eyes, and smil'd at what she saw
In their clear depths, and after that she spake :

2.

" I am the Mother Eve,
    The mother of all flesh.
Glad am I Faith and Love to see,
    And to refresh
    The thirsting of mine eyes
    Ev'n in the midst of Paradise.
With sight of earthly daughter like to thee.
    The primal blessing have I known,
    The primal curse,
    As no one of my race may know ;
    Yet have I learn'd to grow
In faith and trust—to suffer not alone,
    When all the universe
Was nought but darkness and a howling waste,
And all the plan of God seem'd turn'd to naught ;
    When I the mother sought
Beside the dead son's head to lay mine own ;
Nor yet forgat my first-born, whom I thought
The man who should redeem the evil days.

    " Yea, ev'n when chas'd,
Accursèd, from the presence of the Lord,
    Over the Eastern waste,
In the dead time of night he heard

His mother's voice that comforted.
The breast that erstwhile fed
Panted above him, like a bird
Over her young one fallen from the nest,
Whom not her feeble force can raise,
Yet hovereth and cannot rest
All the night season ; when the days
Are hottest, fain would be a shadow for him.
So yearned I, until he found abode,
And built a city in a land,
Remote and dim,
Yet not forgotten of the face of God.
My daughter, in the desert sand
Thy feet may sink,
And thou thirst at the well to drink ;
Yet shalt thou sing
Thy song of wayfaring,
Nor sing it lonely—twain are not alone.
Go then, my children, hand in hand,
Till ye have grown
One spirit, worthy to possess the land."

3.

With mellow fall her voice ceas'd, and she drew
Into the dusky covert of the wood ;
And after she was wholly pass'd away
A voice floated like perfume through the air :

4.

SONG.

" Pleasant is sunshine after rain,
Pleasant the sun ;
To cheer the parched land again,
Pleasant the rain.

" Sweetest is joyance after pain,
Sweetest is joy ;
Yet sorest sorrow worketh gain,
Sorrow is gain."

5.

So died the song,
And once again we heard the wood-doves moan,
The breakers churn the shingles on the shore,
And for a moment were again alone.

But to one point drew all the scattered beams,
And fresher than a waking rose in May,
When from its lips the sun doth kiss the dew,
Upward one came, dividing the dark wood
With subtlest radiance, and our heart was glad.

A space she let the silence of her eyes
Speak for her, ere the wonder of her voice
Brake on us. Lo, the like I never heard,
Save one, that on a summer Sabbath morn,

Lone in the loneliest dell in Kent, I heard
Come with the airs that stir about the dawn—
The nightingale's farewell, so sweet and clear,
She must have wash'd her throat in morning dew,
To still the throb of pain.   In such a voice,
And with such morning sweetness, she began :

6.

" Most sweet, my sister, dost thou know,
 Her who doth call thee so,
 Ev'n Ruth of Moab?   Unto whom the Lord
 Gave dower of joy above her kin ;
 For a great voice she heard
 Within her house in Moab, and again
 On the red Edom hills,
When about sundown, after weeping vain,
Orphah return'd, and only Ruth
Clave to Naomi ; and God enter'd in,
And all her home-sick crying stills,
And the keen natural murmur of her youth.

 " '*Arise and come,*
 Through midnight and through rain,
 Into the sweet cool light of morn,
 And the noontide that ripeneth the corn.'

 " So the Lord call'd me ;
And straightway I arose and went,

And evermore clave to Naomi, she
Whose name is called Bitterness ;
   And ever less and less
Became my kin to me,
   And less and less
The homestead and the village well,
And all my widow'd life I gave
To the thrice widow'd, bearing half her pain,
   In watching tenderness.

"And lo, the Lord had joy in store
For her who only coveted a grave ;
   And more and more
When to my feet the ways were hard,
From the third heaven smiled the Lord,
And sent His angel thence,
To me the alien in the children's land,
With Love for a full recompense.

   " In morning air
Around Beth-Léhem stood the yellow corn,
And I, who hardly glean'd on sufferance there ;
But when that crop was fully garner'd in,
I wan the crown of many a year,
   A mighty thing to win—
A strong man's love, the love that casts out fear.
O sister mine, young, fair, and dear,
If such thou hast, hold it most sure ;

For in this bitter sea of strife
   Which men call *Life*,
   Still to endure
And wait the grave seems all that most
Can hope ; not as in early days
   Before the people lost
The peace God gave them at the first ;
   Yet lost not all
The love of fields and instinct pastoral.

Yea, hold thou love, for at the worst
   That is an anchorage
When north winds howl and all the waters rage."

7.

Bending, she laid a kiss most sisterly
Upon my maid's pure forehead, and so flash'd,
Like gleam of sun on a cloud-blowing day,
Across the wet ripe corn ; and the dim wood
Stay'd with us, and the morning grew to noon.
Then rose a voice, like to the spring of day,
From the dead noon of night, and unto us
Who hearken'd, the words seem'd like to these :

F

8.

SONG.

" Entreat me not
From thy dear side to rove ;
For love uplooks to love,
As earth to heaven above.
　Entreat me not !

" Entreat me not
To turn from following thee
On land or over sea,
Where'er thy foot may be.
　Entreat me not !

" Entreat me not !
For shall I not resign
The kinsfolk that were mine,
And own no God but thine ?
　Entreat me not !

" Entreat me not !
For where 'tis thine to die,
In that far country I
Ensepulchred shall lie.
　Entreat me not !

" Entreat me not !
For God may me desert,

If less than mine thou art,
Or aught but death us part !
Entreat me not ! "

9.

Straightway at the song's ending were we 'ware
Of one, warm-splendid like the south, who mov'd
As used to woodlands, ardent as the glow
Of Syria's noon ; eyes shining from the dusk
Of wondrous hair, tender as eyes of doves
Among the rocks in cedar'd Lebanon ;
Lips like twin flowers, almost one scarlet flower—
A dewdrop scarce had resting-place between ;
And gracious curves of maidenhood, reveal'd,
Through the white raiment that about her clung,
As doth the snow on Hermon's sacred head,
Or the spring glory on the orchard trees.
   So without word we knew whoso it was—
That nameless Shulamite, whose faithfulness
Is writ for ever in the " Song of Songs."

10.

   " Lo, I," she said, " am she,
Whom Solomon the king brought from my home,
Among the vineyards of my northern land,
      That I might be
Another maid to kiss his sacred hand,

And to his hero-guarded chamber come
    At his most kingly pleasure ;
But Lebanon doth rear no crouching slave
    To kiss his garment's hem,
      Nor daughter of Jerusalem
To love dishonour when well purple-clad.

    " And when in boundless measure,
Right royally to make me glad,
    He pour'd his royal treasure,
My sick sad heart pursued the grave ;
Faint grew my soul for fear of sin—
      Swooning, I seem'd to walk within
      The holy calm of cedar temples on
      The sunny slopes of forest Lebanon.

    " No more the perfum'd glooms
      Of Zion's palace rooms,
      Languorous and faint and cool ;
      No more the webs of delicate attire,
      Strange stones, with hearts of fire ;
No more dull eyes and dead burnt-out desire ;
      But gowns of Syrian wool,
      Wov'n by the fireside looms.
      No more the fiery eyes
      Of the Egyptian queen,
But starlight through the arches green,
And west winds singing through the trees,
Fresh from the blue Sidonian seas.

" And One was with me, walking there,
A King of simple men, a manly King,
My King, straight-limb'd and fair ;
Not one who lusteth delicately,
For whom from far men bring
Things pleasing in his sight
To stir the sated gorge of appetite.

" And yet, through pain, held I to purity,
Until again my land God let me see ;
And in no dream I stood
Once more in our dear wood,
And at my side close my belovèd moved—
Ever belovèd, now grown thrice belov'd—
Love shining in our eyes, and we
Bond ever each to each, yet ever free.

" That Love is thus, not less,
Thine eyes, O maid, confess ;
That Faith is victory, thou,
O man, dost surely know."

II.

So ending, through the wood we saw her go,
And somewhere in the shade a song was sung :

12

SONG.

" Floods cannot drown Love's breath,
   It fears not Death's cold wave,
   For Love is strong as Death ;
     But jealousy
  As cruel as the grave.

" ' Where is the gold,' he saith,
   ' Gold that I freely gave ? '
   Nay, Love is strong as Death,
     But Jealousy
  As cruel as the grave.

" No gold can purchase Faith ;   .
   But Love thy soul can save ;
   For Love is strong as Death,
     But Jealousy
  As cruel as the grave."

13.

So underneath the English sky
These ancient lovers pass them by ;
Beneath their feet, that knew so well
The sunburnt plains of Israel
Or high Iranian mountain plain,
The northern grass is soft again,

And England's tender springtime brings
The memories of earlier springs.

There, nurtured in pure Grecian air,
Came Helen, fairest of the fair ;
Andromeda, upon her wrist
The chain-scars Perseus oft had kiss'd ;
And, widow-like in disarray,
Dead Hector's wife Andromache.
These 'neath the fruit-trees blossoming,
Found old-time love in this new spring.

Then three through English woodlands pass
Who knew the touch of English grass—
The crown of love, Queen Guinevere ;
That winsome girl, above whose bier
All youth and wifehood wept in vain,
Queen of our hearts, sweet Lady Jane ;
And Shakespeare's daughter, who doth bring
With her the keys of love and spring.

And longing wistful looks they cast
Upon a love not overpast,
While back the western wind doth bring
The sweetly lingering words they sing ;
And lo, in this wise did they seem
To sing at ending of my dream,
As when from winter wakening
Rings the full chorus of the spring !

14.

SONG.

"Sweet mouth, red lips, broad unwrinkled brow,
Sworn troth, woven hands, holy marriage vow,
Unto us make answer, what is wanting now?
 Love, Love, Love, the whiteness of the snow ;
 Love, Love, Love, and the days of long ago.

" Broad lands, bright sun, as it was of old ;
Red wine, loud mirth, gleaming of the gold ;
Something yet awanting—how shall it be told?
 Love, Love, Love, the whiteness of the snow ;
 Love, Love, Love, and the days of long ago.

" Large heart, true love, service void of sound,
Life trust, death trust, here on English ground,
As in olden story, surely have we found !
 Love, Love, Love, the whiteness of the snow ;
 Love, Love, Love, and the days of long ago."

1884-5.

MY POETESS'S POEM.

My poetess ! whose verses
   Are those pure thoughts of thine,
Whose loyal heart converses
   In words too sweet for rhyme—

I felt thy love this morning
   Come o'er me at my prayer ;
It needed not adorning,
   Nor words to make it fair.

For did I not remember
   The pure His face shall see,
And God in thy heart's chamber
   Dwelleth eternally.

And if the words thou sayest
   Shame my poor poet's art,
How wondrous when thou prayest
   The poems of thine heart.

For somewhere near the flashing
    Of clear green northern seas,
Thou listenest their dashing,
    And writest words like these :

1.

" Far art thou, O belovèd,
    Who art mine own right hand ;
Thou canst not share the beauty
    Of thine own Scottish land ;
Thou canst not hear the love-names
    On the mountains where thou art,
Like everlasting music
    That run within my heart.

2.

" These sunbeams bring no joyance,
    Because they light not thee ;
Most sad, O heart's affiance,
    Is all the sunbright sea.
Yet spite of waves and mountains
    Our lonely hands that part,
Like everlasting music
    Thy love runs in my heart.

3.

" Each day and night there floweth
    The salt tide to the land,

And twice a day it goeth
  Back o'er the waste sea-sand ;
So with a steady current,
  And by a faithful chart,
Like everlasting music
  Thy love runs in my heart.

4.

" Lo ! thou dost hear the wonder
  Of God's voice on the hill,
The icefall's thrilling thunder,
  The after silence still !
Canst hear in that great silence
  That falleth where thou art,
The low sound of the music
  That runneth in my heart ?

5.

" Canst thou, O heart's belovèd,
  Hear evermore the chords ?
Canst feel that thou art lovèd
  Above all force of words ?
And canst thou hear the message
  I send thee where thou art—
Like everlasting music
  Thy love runs in my heart ? "

RIFFEL, VALAIS,
  August 8, 1884.

THAT NOT IMPOSSIBLE SHE.

Lo, in the spring weather,
  Bonnet of dainty size,
  Queen-like, tiara-wise,
Just underneath her
    Red gipsy feather.

Down let the eyes go,
Following the fineness,
The subtle divineness,
The perfection of dressing,
That defines, unexpressing,
  Her maidenly figure.

Wind that so fierce doth blow—
  Blustering weather,
Soften thy rigour,
Thy boisterous vigour
Flee to the hills of the
Young mountain heather,
Ruffle the rills of the
    Still upland valleys ;

Cease thy wild sallies,
    Thy vehement gesture ;
Soft as Ariel's winglet
Caress thou each ringlet,
    Each fold of her vesture ;

Thy rude blowing soften,
See that thy freaks of
    Turbulent playing
Freshen, not roughen
The meadow-sweet cheeks of
This maid who goes Maying
In gracefuller guise than a
    Goddess Diana !

See the ring on her finger,
    Glove-hidden, dainty !
Why will ye linger,
    Maids sweet and twenty ?
None hath design'd such a
    Charming hand wringer ;
Haste ye, and find such a
    Ring for your finger !

Wind that doth bless her too,
    Blowing so faintly,
Thou dost confess her too
    Queenly and saintly ;
Now shall I kiss her too,
    Ever so gently.

1885.

THE YOUNG THINGS IN THINE EYES.

IN the hawthorn arbour out on the green,
　Withdrawn from the people's view,
A man and a maid awhile have been ;
　That is to say—*we two !*

The world is fair all round about,
　The sky is blue to-day ;
On the southward wall are the roses out,
　And the month is the month of May.

The blossoms above are rosily bright ;
　But the shadows are blue and fine,
Where the hawthorn red and the hawthorn white,
　Most lovingly intertwine.

We two are as close as the red and the white—
　'Tis as pleasant here as there ;
And the mad cap dance of the leaf-sieved light
　Never lit on a happier pair.

But yet of the fair things far and near,
   I think that the fairest lies
Hid in a fringèd tent, my dear,
   'Neath the lids of thy sweet eyes.

The rarest of all is never seen
   By folk in the city whirl,
But in secret bower like the Fairy Queen
   Hides the sweet rare heart of a girl.

There's a lambent light in the still sea deeps
   Of a sunless paradise ;
But I love the tender dew that steeps
   The babies in thine eyes.

O small young things of the unknown tongue,
   Whose tale I know so well,
Like a chant by unseen angels sung
   Are the words ye come to tell.

Ye sweet twin babies, in years how old
   Were ye in the land above,
And what angel touch'd your heads with gold,
   And your baby lips with love ?

" O ye," they say, " who are living your life,
   We two shall never grow old,
But shall babies be, when husband and wife,
   Ye are drawing anear the fold.

" Let the love that keeps us young and warm
　　Live in your hearts so true,
That peace may banish the fear of harm
　　While we are abiding with you."

This is the story their silence tells
　　To my heart this summer day,
That shall ring like the pleasant sound of bells
　　When the world is well away.

When we meet at morn by the summer sea,
　　When we part in the moonlight pale,
Never old or cold shall the babies be,
　　Nor ever their smiling fail.

So keep we bright, betide what may,
　　The light in their eyes, my dove,
That sweet and pure they may shine for aye,
　　Those innocent babies of love.

Lo, here in the arbour out on the green
　　Where awhile there sat *we two*,
Neath the hawthorn blossom four have been—
　　The babies—and I—and you !

1885.

O LEMAN LAKE.

O LEMAN Lake, dear Leman Lake,
  Thy beauty knows no change ;
In thee the Savoy Alps still make
  A double mountain range.

All round the shores of Leman Lake
  Shineth the early dew ;
Outstanding lines of poplar break
  Thy plain of steadfast blue.

O'er Territet and Chillon's keep
  No faintest zephyrs blow ;
And terrac'd Vevey lies asleep,
  With vine-stocks all a-row.

Crimson and glorious morning gold
  Deck every vineyard wall ;
The grapes within their sunny fold
  Hang ripe and purple all.

There in the blue, Rhone pushes out
   His snow-fed waters grey;
And there with walnuts girt about
   Lies little Bouveret.

At Evian, lo, the flag of France
   Wooeth the breezes coy,
And through the pines comes furious Drance
   White from the High Savoy.

While over all doth brood the light
   So dear to Leman Lake,
That glimmer of diffus'd delight
   The lawny cloudlets make.

Of old, beneath a sky like this
   Love grew and hate was bred;
And still to-day the lovers kiss,
   And still they mourn the dead.

'Tis long ago since mourner's foot
   Climb'd Jaman's weary road;
Yet exile still is bitter fruit,
   And heavy still its load.

But, Love, when we together go,
   And thy hand holdeth mine,
How limpid Leman's waves will flow,
   How soft the sun will shine!

How the far snows will draw us on,
   The Valais snows I know,
On which the morning sunshine shone
   Many an hour ago.

Yet fair these vineyards round my door,
   Fair this blue inland sea,
Since some one on another shore
   Liveth and loveth me.

How much more fair when her sweet eyes
   Lake Leman's peace shall see,
And all the pleasant land that lies
   'Twixt France and Italy.

1884.

IDYLL OF THE HAYFIELD.

Hey for the haymaking weather!
  Hey for the meadows green!
Scythemen all swinging together,
  Swish of the blades so keen.

There go the ranks of the mowers,
  Sweeping the swathes behind,
Bending as tall meadow flowers
  Bend in a westerly wind.

To the east their heads are inclining
  For a last strong kiss from the sun,
And a draught of his early shining
  Just once ere their life is done.

Dragon-flies hover and shiver
  Over the gnat-haunted pool;
Cows are knee-deep in the river,
  Flicking the flies in the cool.

Stridently down in the meadow
　　Stone upon steel is laid ;
Down where the grass is in shadow
　　Some one is sharpening his blade ;

With hey for the haymaking weather !
　　Hey for the meadows green !
Scythemen all swinging together,
　　Swish of the blades so keen.

Here come the haymaking lasses,
　　Bonneted safe from the sun,
Merrily tossing the grasses,
　　Wild roses every one.

Brown are their faces haymaking,
　　Bright as this summer's day ;
Strong are the arms that are raking
　　And shaking the new-mown hay.

Rare is the haymaking weather,
　　Strong with the strength of June ;
Lasses and lads together,
　　Sing to a haymaking tune.

Singing and swinging and bringing
　　Hay from the meadows green,
Maying and playing and haying,
　　All are most pleasant, I ween.

All in the haymaking weather,
   Lumbering along the ways,
The wains in a row together
   Creak home in the longest days,

With hey for the haymaking **weather !**
   Hey for *the meadows* **green !**
Scythemen all swinging together,
   Swish of the blades so **keen.**

Rattling **and** battering **and** clattering,
   The hay waggons cumber the road ;
Rustling and hustling and bustling,
   The hay-mow swallows the load.

But somehow **the haymaking riot**
   Dies into **silence soon,**
For I am possessed with the **quiet**
   And drowse **of** the afternoon.

And in the dim hay-loft, a-glimmer
   With motes in the slant sunbeam,
If the world gets dimmer and dimmer
   Who shall chide if **I** sleep and dream,

Of the lazy haymaking weather,
   The drowsy meadows green,
Scythemen all swinging together,
   Swish of the blades so keen ?

1885.

I CANNOT SEND THEE GOLD.

I CANNOT send thee gold
    Nor silver for a show ;
Nor are there jewels sold
    One half so dear as thou.

No daffodil doth blow
    In this dull winter time,
Nor purple violet grow
    In so unkind a clime.

To-day I have not got
    One spray of meadow-sweet,
Nor blue forget-me-not
    My posy to complete.

Yet none of these can claim
  So much goodwill as you ; .
Their lips put not to shame
  Cowslip and oxlip too.

But joy I'll take in this,
  Pleasure more sweet than all,
If thou this book but kiss
  As Love's memorial.

1883.

O HEART'S DELIGHT.

O Heart's Delight, on whose love-lorn grey eyes
   And sweet red carven lips a dower of pain
Weighs heavily to-day—dumb sorrow lies
   So close about thine heart, thou canst not gain
The wreath of joy that is sad sorrow's crown.
   Ah, love, thine eyes pursue me ! look they thus
Heavy with tears that will not fall adown,
   Drowned in a waveless sorrow ?   Unto us
Parting is not mere loosing of two hands,
     Or murmuring of good-byes ;
But twaining souls, and breaking body bands,
   And silencing life's sweetest harmonies.

II.

Do I not know the ache in thy sick heart,
   As on thine empty palm thy fingers close ;

And these thy lips, that feel the March winds' smart
   Miss sore the kiss whose sweetness no one knows?
Yea, love, my love, this wind is bitter cold;
   About thee draw thy shawl's soft fold azùre,
And in thy bosom's screen'd recess withhold
   Thy maiden flower of love, all fair and pure;
For we have lost but what our eyes have seen,
     Yet kept securely all
Love's country still untroubled and serene,
   And closer drawn our union mystical.

III.

I linger by the fen's uncertain edge,
   And watch last year's tall tufted rushes sway,
And the dry pennons of the rustling sedge
   On either side the long dim waterway.
The moor-birds call responsively, and sweep
   In viewless circles, wailing as they go;
And in the distant pasture-lands the sheep
   To their own lambs bleat plaintively and low.
All is most cool and still, when suddenly
     A low sweet murmur fills
My pulses like the springtide from the sea—
   " *Thine I am now, and all thine when God wills.*"

IV.

Then golden grows the sudden pall of dark,
    For a fair head lies on my breast, and all
The grim world's grief and troublous daily cark
    Into the night's concave doth noiseless fall,
And dear arms cling about mine aching head,
    And from that soft touch pain and trouble fly ;
The heart's long weary ache is comforted
    By touch of lips, the sweetest under sky.
Ah, Heart's Delight, is any love like our's,
        Making dull absence seem
Like Presence' self, whose sacred bond empowers
    Our souls to meet in world-forgetting dream ?

V.

Doth not the northern wind bring fitfully
    Imagined sense of sweet from a far land
Unto this marge of lazy southern sea ?
    Nay, too remote are brown flint-strewn sea sand,
And wistful sighing pines high on the down ;
    These golden belts that ring the forest ways,
Green bayonetted gorse and heather brown,
    Too distant from yon driftèd city haze,
And bursting blossoms of a slower spring.
        No winds that wandering go
Can wafts of fragrance from the nor'land bring
    To this clear loneliness of morning glow.

VI.

As unkiss'd mountains, underneath the star
  Of sunless January, hunger for
The sungod's horses and his flaming car ;
  As on the waste wide sand-dunes by the shore
Lieth all night and longeth for the tide,
  A stranger from the waste wide sea ;
Or as the ocean's self, unglorified
  By sun or moon, swayeth so wistfully
'Twixt sad sea wave and sadder interval ;—
    So uncheered darkness lies
Close round my soul, until there break through all,
  The shadowy radiance of thy twilight eyes.

VII.

O mellow rain upon the clover tops ;
  O breath of morning blown o'er meadow-sweet ;
Lush apple blooms, from which the wild bee drops
  Inebriate ; O hayfield scents, my feet
Scatter abroad some morning in July ;
  O wild-wood odours of the birch and pine,
And heather breaths from great red hill-tops nigh,
  Than olive sweeter, or Sicilian vine ;—
Not all of you, nor summer lands of balm,
    Not blest Arabia,
Nor coral isles in seas of tropic calm,
  All Heart's Desire unto my heart can draw.

VIII.

O scent of sea on dreaming April morn,
   Borne landward on a steady blowing wind ;
O August breeze, o'er leagues of rustling corn,
   Wafts of clear air from uplands left behind,
And outbreath'd sweetness of wet wallflower bed ;
   O set in Mid-May depth of orchard close,
Tender germander blue, geranium red ;
   O express'd freshness of sweet briar rose ;—
Too gross, corporeal, absolute are ye !
      Ye help not to define
   That subtle fragrance, delicate and free,
   Which like a vesture clothes this love of mine.

1884.

THE MIDNIGHT OF THE YEAR.

AGAINST the pane I press my brow,
  And wonder in the midnight cold
What time of year is with us now—
  Not yet the New, nor quite the Old.

No wind doth stir ; it is so still
  That I can hear a mile away
An outlaw dog upon the hill
  Pursue with pain his swift-foot prey.

So dark, I hardly see the ash
  Against the sky uplift its arms ;
But far away the watch-lights flash
  In solitary upland farms.

Behind, the fire hath wan'd to red,
  And one by one the embers fade ;
While dimly shineth by my bed
  The lamp beneath its tripled shade.

Though through the dark no bells have peal'd,
    Jarring the air with brazen might,
Not all forsaken is the field,
    Nor tenantless the year's midnight.

Across the silent plain of air
    Stalk four and twenty silent ghosts—
The phantoms of my years that were,
    Dead in the drear December frosts.

And yet I fear them not—they come,
    Nor shall their race till doomsday fail ;
They go, the units in my sum,
    If long or short be then my tale.

Why should I fear ?   They bring me joy
    And grief in almost equal store.
Ah ! should not then each year enjoy
    Grateful acceptance more and more.

Why should I fear, if in the field
    In the sweet spring I sow the corn,
Into my barns to store the yield
    Ere unto midnight turns the morn ?

I think that surely that dear grace
    Which to my life our Lord did lend,
Will make the ghosts a happier race
    I turn adrift at the year's end.

'Tis now the **New Year on the earth** ;
   And to **a maiden in the south**
I call amid her festal mirth,
   And bend to kiss her sweet-set mouth.

My girl, I could not love thee more
   Wert **thou my** wedded wife yestreen,
Or did we hearken at our door
   The bells divide the midnight keen.

Yet though thou seemest half divine,
   A flower from Heaven's garden **sent,**
One day thou shalt be wholly mine
   In the sweet land of Well-Content.

Though now **the flowers** all hidden **are,**
   The lilies **sunken in the** mere,
Thine heart **is treasure** sweeter **far**
   Than **all** the gardens **of the year.**

1883-4.

EVEN SONG.

IN the even sings the voice,
    Soft and slow,
Of the maiden of my choice :
    Very low
    Singeth she
Ballads mystic, carols old,
Fragments graceful, sweet, or bold,
    All for me.

Bliss of love's full thoughtedness
    Swift doth rise ;
Haze of unforgetfulness
    . Dims mine eyes ;
    And I see
Precious hopes and bitter fears
Down the vista of the years
    That shall be.

H

Thou and I shall ever cling
      Yet more near,
And the darkness shall us bring
      Naught to fear ;
      We shall go
Ringed by evil tongues of spite,
Shapes that wander in the night
      To and fro.

Through the darkness and the noise
      Lo, I hear
Thrilling upward a sweet voice ;
      In mine ear
      Doth its tone
Tell me all I yearn to know
Up the world-way as I go
      Not alone.

1884.

LOVE AND KNOWLEDGE.

Since I have loved my love
　　A year or so,
What have I done to prove
　　My love doth grow
　　From less to more?

Since I have seen her grace
　　Make glad the home,
Sweeten the household ways,
　　Hath it become
　　A richer store? .

Lo! I have marked her face
　　Men's eyes enthrall—
Fairest in every place,
　　Yet she through all
　　Was still my maid.

Love I her less or more
　　That I have seen

And learn'd her deep love lore,
  And with her been
   Through shine and shade?

Can it be less, when I,
  In awe and fear,
Have stood her white soul nigh
  As it drew near
   And talked with God?

Aye, more a thousand fold
  My love hath grown,
Older yet never old,
  Good seed well sown
   In fruitful sod.

As knowledge grows in me
  Love keeps the pace;
And never may'st thou see
  One win the race
   Nor lag behind.

Love keepeth that fair land
  Knowledge hath won,
And these two hand in hand
  Till set of sun
   Thou still shalt find.

1884.

BY THE SEA.

THE peace of waveless rest is on the sea.
I hear no sound, albeit I listen till
Ears ache with silentness and silence' self
Becomes a sound—only the hidden sough
Of hill-brook yearning towards the primal sea,
Weary of granite hills and clefted glens.

   Peace in my tired heart even as I watch
The surge of hills serrate against the sky,
Emulous of the steady polar star ;

   For this my love is with me and her voice
Dwells in mine ear, and in my central heart
The memory of To-day is throbbing strong.

   I feel her blissful kiss upon my lips
Say " *Benedicite.*"   My soul goes home
That way, as a belated bird, aweary,
Nestles at last by his homekeeping mate.

   'Tis she and I against the whelming world ;
All else falls back—scarce to be wondered at—
Faintly at most, hardly of interest

Sufficient for a question, but as one
Might say, " What ship is that whose pulsing wheels
We hear out there i' the west ? "   And yet withal
As meaningless to me as a dog's howl
Far heard at dead of night when no wind blows.

   That is her casement's narrow vacant square.
Lo, see, a light shines from it, and I know
All joy within ; without, the empty air,
And the unfriendly sea and I alone.

   But in the west I see Love's planet sweet,
Regnant above the everlasting hills ;
And then, with heart love-heavy, home I go.

1883.

"THERE WAS AE FLOUR."

THERE was ae flour in a fair garden,
    Where the lilac blossom blooms cheerily ;
" Fairest and rarest ever was seen,"
    Sing the merle and laverock merrily.

Watered o' dew i' the earliest morn,
    Lilac blossom blooms cheerily ;
Bield aboot wi' a sweet hawthorn,
    Where the merle and lark sing merrily.

Wha will pu' this flour o' the flours ?
    Lilac blossom blooms cheerily ;
Wha hae for aye to grace their bours
    Where the merle and lark sing merrily ?

1883.

COR CORDIUM.

In old sad days when I withdrew me
  To watch thee from afar,
Thou wast a goddess fair unto me,
  But distant as they are.

From earthy dross mine ore refining,
  I felt thy clear eyes draw
Truth's minted gold, and their still shining
  Bind all men to their law—

A law as pure as white lake lilies,
  But cold as snow is cold ;
The gold hearts of the daffodillies
  Seem'd more of love to hold.

And yet each one that knows thee knoweth
  That strange sweet power of thine,
To make man's heart a fire that gloweth
  Fiercer than furnace shine.

Thou art no goddess, but a maiden
  Whom God hath made too fair;
Thou comest to a heart deep laden
  Like soft sea-scented air.

When in the darkness I remember
  Thee smile with quiet eyes,
The winter midnight of December
  On a May morn doth rise.

'Tis long ago since thou hast taken
  The sleeping love in me,
And made my whole life to awaken
  To one sole thought of thee.

And now to thee, my life's liege lady,
  What good gift can I bring?
Is not my whole heart's treasure ready
  To be mine offering?

Yea, all of old to maiden given   .
  Thy knight shall give to thee,
Though now most rare on this side heaven,
  Love, worship, fealty.

1883.

WEALTH OF ROSES.

WEALTH of roses hast thou **sent,**
   Lying bright,
All in mellow osier pent,
   Red and white.

Blue forget-me-nots, the best
   Thou did'st send—
Fern encircled, **dew caress'd,**
   O my friend !

Sent too, store of garden grace,
   Cultured **sweets—**
Guardian Dryads of the **place,**
   Marguerites ;

Bringing wafts **of country air**
   To my rooms,
Shaming all my foolish care,
   And my glooms.

Words are all I can return   .
　　For thy grace ;
Yet thy love shall surely earn
　　Happy days.

1883.

LOVE LIETH LOWLY.

A NEW SONG TO AN OLD TUNE.

Low in the morning, Love lieth weeping,
  Wayworn and weary, ready to die;
All his bright arrows gone from his keeping,
  Broken his pinions—how shall he fly?
Through his fair ringlets rough winds are sweeping,
  Low his head in the dust doth lie.
    Maidens, sing this sad song slowly,
    " Love's head lieth lowly."

They have forgotten, all the gay rovers,
  Gifts that he gave them summers ago;
All of them gone now, half-hearted lovers,
  Fair weather friends in the winter that go.
Cold is the raiment young Love that covers—
  Woven webs of the drifted snow.
    Maidens, sing this sad song slowly,
    " Love's head lieth lowly."

Through the white snow-wreath cometh a maiden,
  Up in her arms she taketh the boy.
See the soft mantle Love is arrayed in,
  Never again to suffer annoy;
Unto her house she goeth Love-laden,
  Holding Love in her heart of joy.
    Sing no more a sad song slowly,
    Love's head lies not lowly.

1884.

A YEAR TO-NIGHT.

To-NIGHT I touched thy hand, my dear,
In the dead winter of the year;
To-night saw first eyes grey and clear,
      A year ago.

Only a year! but if it were
Ten ages more, could it transfer
Or alter by a single hair
      This love we know?

To-night into my life there came
Of Love and Faith the equal flame;
My very soul was not the same   ·
      A year ago.

And yet our spirits met, I wot,
In some prenatal field of thought—
Clasp'd hands, and then a while forgot
      On earth below.

Didst thou recall a lifetime spent
In mutual knowledge well content,
When all thy soul to mine outwent
    A year ago?

I think that in the treasure-house
Whence souls are taken, God allows
Each unborn soul to choose a spouse
    And forth to go.

But sometimes in the crowded mart
The wedded pair are torn apart—
'Twas well I knew whose twin thou wert
    A year ago!

1883.

OUR LADY OF THE WOODS.

I WILL show you a tree on the edge of the wood,
At its foot the lady fern breaketh in spray,
And ten times a day it changeth its mood,
Like a wayward maiden, grave or gay.
  Aye, our birch is a beauty—I wonder now
If you would think it was like a girl—
Lissom and graceful, a girl we know?
  Well, you never *had* any eyes ; a pearl
Might lie a long time in an oyster for you,
Unless it should stick in your Philistine throat !
  Oh, you " *see what I'm driving at now,*" you do,
And you ask, " *What resemblance are you to note ?* "

First, then, you may mark the grace of its curve,
And the subtle spring of the airy top,
All instinct with life to each delicate nerve,
And in each curl'd leaf a crystalline drop,
That sprinkles your face as you brush it aside—
Then that springtime scent in the morning air
Makes you stay unawares the swing of your stride,
And take time to admire my beauty there.

Can you see it now? at the fir-wood's end,
You'll catch its gleam like a fairy's wand,
Grey and clear like the eyes of my friend.

It is ringed with purple and delicate band
Of russet and brown and marvellous grey,
And one gets, here and there on its silvery stem,
Wherever the bark has curl'd away,
Shy glimpse of a dainty underhem.
　　But I cannot see it—it stood just here—
What is this?　Our birch—in a wrack of trees!
It must have gone with the storm of last year
That swept so strong from the western seas
And wasted the country side.　Well, it must be so;
But yet while my Dryad remaineth to me,
This storm-racked year, it is joy to know,
Brought a love that is better than flower or tree.

1884.

NIGHT BY SUILVEN.

A WEEK ago I heard the hum
　　Of Pleasure's languid multitude,
　　Over the grass to where I stood
From the gay park's long turmoil come.

A week ago I saw the glare
　　Upon a hundred dancers fall;
　　I stood apart and watched it all,
Nor found I aught in which to share.

Here morning draws to afternoon,
　　And afternoon to eventide;
　　And now the shimmering cloudlets hide
Intenser splendours of the moon.

But from her bonds she breaketh soon,
　　And builds a fairy bridge of light,
　　That marks a pathway shining bright
Across the narrows of Loch Fewn.

The ripples break just out of reach—
    Beneath, the hasty river brawls ;
    And, softer than the Kirkaig falls,
Whispers the wind too low for speech.

The lake lies underneath the hill,
    The hill scarce underneath the skies,
    So instant and abrupt doth rise
Wierd Suilven's ancient pinnacle.

Here, then, 'tis passing good to bide,
    For dearer to the quiet mind
    Than fashion's festival, I find
The hamlet by the sea-loch's side.

ASSYNT, SOUTHERLAND,
    1881.

FROM TWO WINDOWS.

This window looketh toward the west,
  And o'er the meadows grey
Glimmer the snows that coldly **crest**
  The hills of Galloway.

The winter broodeth all between—
  In every furrow lies;
Nor is there aught of summer green,
  Nor blue of summer **skies.**

Athwart the dark grey rainclouds flash
  The sea-bird's sweeping wings,
And through the stark and ghostly ash
  The wind of winter sings.

The purple woods are dim with rain,
  The cornfields **dank and bare;**
And eyes **that** look for golden **grain**
  Find only stubble there.

But when I to the window turn
   That fronts the southern plain,
Small sign of winter I discern,
   Or cloud-rack fierce with rain.

Sunshine is not more clear in June,
   Nor August sky more blue;
Not otherwise on summer noon
   Looketh our guardian yew.

And there in leafage never sere
   Stand all the solemn pines;
Nor fresher in the spring appear
   Their melancholy lines.

Dark green against the southern sky
   Their shaggy tops are seen;
The flooded meadow-levels lie
   All silver-grey between.

Thus light and dark and dark and light
   So near together come,
That you may hold them both in sight
   From one small-window'd room.

But while I write, behold the night
   Comes slowly blotting all,
And o'er grey waste and meadow bright
   The gloaming shadows fall.

From all the quiet lattices
  Dim lights are shining soon,
And through the cross-bars of the trees
  Breaketh the wading moon.

1884.

JUNE RAIN IN WALES.

GOLDENER than gold's clear self,
Above the purpling mountain mass the sun
Doth hang, mist-mellow in the even-shine;
Higher, the level curtain of the rain—
Soft summer rain, that blesseth where it falls—
Lets drop two sun-illumin'd folds of shower
Over yon dim blue western promontory—
The folk here call it Lleyn.   Seen hence it seems
A chain of islands like our Hebrides,
Adream amid the rain-still'd northern sea.

　　And now, O love, as thy life circles mine,
And thy dear influence, like the blessed rain,
Stilleth and purifieth the sea's surge,
So is the barren, lone, unquiet sea
Bound by the bands of habitable land,
Still'd by the gentle falling of the rain.

BELOW CADER IDRIS,
　　1884.

A CHRISTMAS GREETING.

A GREETING kind to thee, my **friend**,
  To thee a blithe good-morrow;
And whatsoe'er He doth thee send,
  God send thee never sorrow.

For all good men this Christmas-tide,
  Good girls and they together,
About the fire sit side by side
  To spite the winter weather.

The wind about the missel-bush
  Shakes every waxen berry;
And while it makes the maidens blush,
  It makes the men a-merry.

And while upon this pleasant earth
  Live men both good and jolly,
I wot they'll save for Christmas mirth
  The yule-log and the holly.

And if for lack of city lore
  The verses seem but homely,
I rede thee pardon them the more
  That thou thyself art comely.

1883.

FALSE AND TRUE.

I.

My soul, what doth this triple promise mean,
  This vow by men and angels heard,
    By God enregistered,
To love, to honour, and to keep my Queen?

Ah, many a pair before the altar kneel,
  To whom the sacred words that bless
    Are far more meaningless
Than the hill-echo when their joy-bells peal.

II.

I hear the woman's voice ring clear and true,
  With high heart-service in its tone,
    She gives to him alone
Her store of all love's golden revenue—

To him who brings foul heart unpurified,
   Selfish and cruel as the grave,
     The false heart of the knave,
To match the fair perfection of his bride.

III.

Or shallow heart and selfish, giveth she,
   And thinketh to herself, " Behold,
     All things are got for gold,
And wonderful shall my adorning be ! "

Yet thinketh not, poor fool, that purity
   And truth are not yet bought for gold,
     And happiness not sold
For all the wealth of regal argosy.

IV.

My God, was this the marriage meant by Thee,
   This union of the foul and fair ?
     Can such pollution bear
Thine Eden stamp of love eternally ?

And dost Thou smile approval from the skies,
   Or evil things of darkness leap,
     Where, in the glimmering deep,
Dwelleth Beelzebub, the Prince of Flies ?

Nay, no such marriage Thine, for Thou dost bless
  The Love and Truth and equal yoke,
    That bind Thy faithful folk
By two and two in bands of stedfastness.

V.

So Love is not lip-service, nor is Faith
  A fair-wind helmsman who can steer
    Only where skies are clear,
But fainteth in the murky chasm of Death.

Therefore to love her ever is not hard—
  To love her *not*, as possible
    As that the ambient sea
Should cease the precinct of our isle to guard.

VI.

Like one who, half awaking in the dawn,
  And turning into well-known arms,
    Nestleth from reach of harms
In that beloved haven safe withdrawn ;

So in the shelter of a mutual trust
  Shall we abide, and closer draw
    These sacred bonds, whose law
Is Love undying, though ourselves be dust.

1884.

A FAR CRY.

FROM THE ALPS TO ARGYLE.

A FAIR far land about thee lies,
　Cool'd by the salt lake's breeze;
Thou see'st through great tear-clouded eyes
　The wash of Scottish seas.

With heart to Alpine snows anear,
　From some small hill church bare
Thou liftest to the All-Father
　A maiden's simple prayer.

These thousand miles can not divide
　Thy well-belov'd from thee;
He hearkeneth, silent at thy side,
　The sea-waves' litany.

With thee he marks the white cloud caps
　Fleck all the sunlit land;
His feet, behind the ebb-tide's lapse,
　Make lightnings in the sand.

He hears, above the tinkling bells
   Of cattle pasturing
High on the parchèd Alpine fells,
   The Inver church bells ring.

Steep slopes of dazzling sunlit snow,
   Cleaving the dark-blue sky ;
Or Monte Rosa, all aglow,
   O'erhanging Italy,

Hide not these misty mountain tops
   Drench'd in cool drifts of rain,
The brown-sailed fishing craft that drops
   Down to the western main.

For all the banners of the mist
   About the summits furl'd,
The ledges by the sun first kiss'd,
   This cold white glacier world,

Not of themselves are loveliest,
   But by dear hopes that rise
That all these things may one day rest
   In the Sabbath of thine eyes.

LOVE IS THE TRUE GOLD.

HERE is fine gold for thee
　　For thine adorning,
Sent for the love of thee
　　On Christ's birth morning.

Wear it for Faith's sake,
　　For the work that bought it ;
Wear it for my sake,
　　And the love that thought it.

Love is the true gold,
　　Richest of trover ;
What is the wife's gold ?—
　　Husband and lover !

OBER ENGADIN,
　　1884.

AMONG SEPTEMBER SNOW.

At home 'tis sunny September,
   Though here 'tis a waste of snows,
So bleak that I scarce remember
   How the scythe through the cornland goes.

With an aching heart I wander
   Through the cold and curvèd wreaths,
And dream that I see meander
   Brown burns amid purple heaths.

That I hear the stags on the mountains
   Bray loud in the early morn,
And that scarlet gleams by the fountains
   The red-berried wild-rose thorn.

Very solemn the peaks of the Valais
   Through the broken storm-clouds show,
By the sun made magically
   Whiter than whitest snow.

The dome of soaring Mischabel
　　Shines in a misty dream ;
The Weisshorn and pinnacled Gabel
　　Reign in the west supreme ;

While o'er the White Tooth and the Brothers
　　Ariseth, accursèd and lorn,
God's wedge that divided the others,
　　The marvellous Matterhorn.

Yet scarce can my hungry heart pardon
　　The mountains for being so fair ;
I had liefer behold a garden,
　　And a maiden that resteth there

All under a red thorn's shading,
　　A queen on a rustic throne—
And an English twilight fading
　　On the garden, not alone !

1884.

A CHRISTMAS SONG FOR A LADY.

I.

No song of lark nor blithesome bird
About our winter land is heard,
   So I must tune no serious strain,
   Nor rack my brow for epics vain ;
But while the snows are drifting white,
In cosiest corner will I write
     Some dainty lines for a lady.

II.

" *Goodwill to all who have goodwill,*
To him that hath be given still !"
   And he the angels' vision sees
   Through all the veilèd centuries ;
So weighty words are lightly said,
As gold is wrought in daintiest braid
     In winsome wise for a lady.

III.

A song that bears no dirge of pain
Rings out from English bells again,
  By shepherds heard beneath the fold,
  The glad old song that is not old ;
And I, the echo it doth leave,
Afar from English gladness weave
    In graceful guise for a lady.

IV.

To all to whom the cross is now
The crown awaits the weary brow ;
  Like His, that babe whose wondrous birth,
  In Bethlehem made glad the earth ;
And all my heart is glad, I wot—
Or part is glad and part is not—
    As knoweth well this lady.

V.

For sad songs may be lightly sung,
And gladsome harps on willows hung,
  And days are days and years are years,
  And joy lies near the spring of tears ;
And so as bond for life-long debt,
A thoughtful word or two I set
    In Christmas key for a lady.

MALOJA, UPPER ENGADINE,
  Christmas, 1884.

A WINTER MESSAGE FROM THE HIGH ALPS.

TO GEORGE MILNER.

To you, O friend, who keep a heart
    Unchilled by any snows ;
To you from one who stands apart
    A spring of kindness flows.

From Alpine snows and granite rocks
    I reach revering hands,
Warm with a gratitude that mocks
    These winter-buried lands.

I see you homeward slowly come
    And outside shut the day,
Silence the city's dreary hum
    And put the world away.

And I that have no resting-place
  On hearth for foot of mine,
Turn very wistfully my face
  To watch your hearth-fire shine.

And all my heart goes over seas,
  Though I stay here alone,
To share its sweet observances
  And graceful duties done.

And with my hearth-fire all unmade,
  My home life yet to be,
I sadly watch the sunset fade
  On purple Italy ;

Yet see above the glacier snow
  The full-orb'd promise rise ;
And living love none else may know
  Shine from unfathom'd eyes.

1884.

HAST THOU SEEN? HAST THOU KNOWN?

Hast thou seen the glamour that follows
　　The falling of summer rain—
The mystical blues in the hollows,
　　The purples and greys on the plain?

Hast thou seen the moonlight shining
　　On the fair four cantons' sea,
While all thy heart was pining
　　For two eyes' still mystery?

Hast thou known desire that groweth
　　More wordless and fiercely calm,
Fann'd by the wind that bloweth
　　Soft from the lands of palm?

How wilder than forests Etruscan,
　　Sweeter than Lombard vines,
Softer than vocables Tuscan
　　Heard on the Appennines,

Is the faith that doth not evanish
Under the glare of the day ;
Faith that the night cannot banish—
As deep as the Milky Way,

As clear with wonderful lustre,
As far above earthly jars,
As the Pleiades' glimmering cluster,
The sweetest among the stars.

1884.

NEW RHYME AND OLD REASON.

(WRITTEN IN LEWIS CARROL'S "RHYME? OR REASON?")

Low down among the summer grass,
We two, a lover and his lass,
List the old rhymes of "*breeze,*" and "*trees,*"
And the wind on the level meadow leas.

Dear old-time rhymes of "*love*" and "*dove,*"
Heard in the branches high above,
Never in days gone by were ye
Sung of a love more fair than she.

Half sad, all glad, on this mad page
I rhyme of a love, rhymes cannot gauge ;
While wild rose leaves fall tenderly
Over words that hide what Love can be.

JUNE 14, 1884.

SONG FOR BRIDE-DAY MORNING.

WHITE as early roses, girt by daffodillies,
  Gleam the feet of maidens, moving rhythmically,
  Roses of the mountains, flowers of the valley,
Hill rose and plain rose and white vale lilies.

Dewy in the meadow lands, clover blossoms mellow
  Lift their heads of red and white to the bride's adorning;
  Sweetly in the sky-realms all the summer morning,
Joyeth the skylark and calleth his fellow.

In the well-known precincts, lo the wilding treasure
  Glows for marriage merriment in my sweetheart's
    gardens,
  Welcoming her joy-day, tenderest of wardens—
Heart's pride and love's life and all eyes' pleasure.

Bride among the bridesmaids, lily clad in whiteness,
  She cometh to the twining none may twain in sunder ;
  While to marriage merriment wakes the organ's thunder,
And the Lord doth give us all His heavenly brightness.

Then like early roses, girt by daffodillies
  Goes the troop of maidens, moving rhythmically,
  Roses of the mountains, flowers of the valley,
Hill rose and plain rose and white vale lilies.

1884.

FORGET AND REMEMBER.

THE March wind piercing keen,
Scourging the white highways,
Parching the springing green—
These fitful vexing days,
    O love, do thou forget.

Days of clear sky above
And spring flowers underfoot,
The bursting bud of Love,
And promise of Love's fruit,
    Remember thou, O love.

Cold days of clouded sky,
And hours of shadowed heart,
When one would vainly try
Awhile to stay apart,
    Do thou, O love, forget.

The gold without alloy
Of Faith and Love supreme,

The pure unsullied joy
In waking or in dream,
   O love, remember thou.

The fear of others' thought,
The hardly brooked restraint,
A passing strangeness wrought
By pride's unkindly taint,
   O love, do thou forget.

Those eyes from which shone out
The utter trust of each,
That inner joy no doubt
Or surface storm can reach,
   Remember thou, O love.

Though Memory's wells o'erflow
With undrawn draughts of joy,
Most hard 'tis now to know
What motes did us annoy—
   So, love, do thou forget.

But love of sacred days,
Sweet rest beneath one roof,
Two hearts one song of praise,
Love, of God's love the proof,
   O love, remember thou.

All that thou wouldst not let
Come near our own bright hearth,
    O love, do thou forget !
A love like heaven on earth,
    O love, remember thou !

1885.

A TRANSCRIPT FROM THE "SONG OF SONGS."

THE MAID.

I.

BETTER than cup of fine gold from the south
Fill'd with wine's treasure-trove,
Are these thy lips. So kiss me, love,
O kiss me, with the kisses of thy mouth.

2.

Behold, the damsels love thee, O belovèd,
Because thy name is fair,
And of sweet odour, like the air
Of delicate nard that clings about thy head.

3.

Draw us, thou strong one, for our hearts incline
To thee. Within his hall
The king hath brought me; but *thy* call
I'll follow, for thy love is more than wine.

4.

Most true, O daughters of the hill of Zion,
No maiden lily white
Am I ; yet comelier in his sight
Than Kedar's tents, curtains of Solomon.

5.

I kept my brethren's vines though I was fair,
For hot their anger was —
Ah ! look not on me— for, alas !
Of mine own vineyard have I had no care.

6.

Tell me, O thou for whom my soul hath love,
Where feeds thy flock ? at noon
Where rests ? for why should I as one
Lone and forgot, among thy fellows rove.

CHORUS.

If this thy good thou wilt not know,
 Thou all too simple maid,
Afar among the rocks
 Feed thou thy flocks ;
By the low earthen cotes
Where shepherds tend their goats,
 By hill and hollow
 The sheep-track follow ;
And in queen's raiment be no more arrayed.

THE KING.

1.

Unto my charger
Lo I compare thee,
Chief of the horses
Southward that bare thee,
Guarded and warded,
Girt round by heroes,
In my state chariot,
Gift of the Pharaohs.

2.

Comely thy cheeks are,
Jewels adorn them ;
Chains on thy fair neck,
There thou hast worn them ;
Chains the king gave thee,
His goldsmiths made them,
Studded with bell-tassels,
Silversmiths weighed them.

THE MAID.

1.

While yet the king sat in his banquet hall
    My spikenard scented sweet,
    And I was glad ; but when his feet
Drew near, drooping it hung and scentless all.

2.

To me a bunch of pleasant myrrh thou art,
  My well-beloved, that rests,
  Lying all night between my breasts
Stirr'd by the love-sick pulses of my heart.

3.

" To what is my belovèd like," say I,
  " In whom I take delight ? "
  A spray of henna, red and white,
Among the vines in sunny Engedi.

1882.

AFTER CLOUD THE SUNSHINE.

I.

QUIET are the woods, and dumb
   Are the wood-dove's notes ;
Honey-bees have hush'd their hum,
   Birds their merry throats.

Blossoms of the orchard trees,
   Nipp'd by morning frost,
Flutter on the bitter breeze,
   Life and freshness lost.

Dust doth dim the yellow gold
   Of the wayside gorse ;
Harebells droop upon the wold,
   Spring hath lost her force.

Stay'd the first glad burst of power,
   Check'd the mounting sap ;
Sweetheart Spring herself doth cower
   In Dame Winter's lap.

II.

Beating down the crested waves
  On the great sea plain,
Over fields and towns and graves,
  Drives the welcome rain.

All the chill and listless leaves,
  Feeble frosted folk,
Sudden smiting tempest reaves
  From the creaking oak.

O'er the garden ways are strown
  Spring's untimely wrack ;
Leaves and flowers and branches blown
  Line the forest track.

III.

This is how the summer came,
  Came with bursting hail,
Racking thunder, instant flame,
  Fierce Atlantic gale.

Yesterday 'twas doubtful spring,
  Heaven of arid grey ;
Day of storm doth summer bring,
  Lo ! 'tis June to-day.

Here to-day is summer's prime,
　　New joy in the trees ;
Sapphire-hearted summer time,
　　Sky, and bluer seas.　　·

1885.

.

HARRY OWEN'S BOOK,

BEING

POET ECHOES

IN

WILD WALES.

" Blow bugle, answer echoes."

[Written in days of rain for the Inn Album at Pen-y-Gwryd, in North Wales, to supply spaces left unfilled by certain poets who of late sojourned there—the Prophet of the Lamentation, the Clerk of Oxenford, the Incomprehensible, the Lordly One, the Democrat of the Earthly Paradise, the Master, the Protean Celt, and the Demoniac Clothed.]

HARRY OWEN'S BOOK.

" I came to Pen-y-Gwryd, a-larking with my betters,
  A mad wag and mad poet, both of them men of letters,
  Which two ungrateful parties, for the care of them I took,
  Have set me writing verses in Henry Owen's book."

                                        T. HUGHES.

  Pen-y-Gwryd, Caernarvonshire.

THIRTY YEARS.

" A voice shall cry in the latter days."

I HAVE not looked for thirty years
    Upon thy humble roof, mine inn ;
Yet, though my voice has tuned the spheres,
    I rest in thee with no disdain.

When in the school's familiar hum,
    The little pontiffs watch my nod,
How often doth the whisper come,
    "How sweet to tread the Cambrian sod."

Ah, thirty years ! how much they change,
  Besides the unquiet heart of man !
How many ghosts through Hades range,
  Who walk'd the earth when ye began.

There were no flakes upon these locks,
  No crafty crowsfeet round mine eyes,
My phrases pointed not the jokes
  Of editors more smart than wise.

No church anathemas were hurl'd,
  Unheard were then Philistia's jeers—
Ah me ! what changes have the world
  And I not seen in thirty years.

But here no sickening discord stills
  The music of the steady stars ;
The winds upon the moon-blanch'd hills
  Joy not in theologic wars.

And in the freedom of mine inn,
  I should not wonder if I am
A trifle nearer to my kin,
  Than isled in esoteric calm.

But still the greatest thoughts are hid
  And nurtured by the reverent few ;
By frantic shriek the mass is led,
  Though I in peace possess the true.

Yet though they seek not what I sought,
   With joy a younger people hears,
What wisdom it hath been my lot
   To reach through pain in thirty years.

FORMOSA ACERRIMAQUE.

By Catullus Oxoniensis.

O SWEETEST of sad maids,
Saddest of sweet maids,
    Euphrosyne's daughter !
In peinture I limn thee,
In poesy hymn thee,
    Beloved of Erato !

Dionysian plethora
Pour from the amphora,
    Sweet Welsh Ganymede ;
And thou'lt have a lyric—
A chaunt neoteric,
    By a poet indeed.

Hail, gracefullest Hebe,
Whoever you may be !
    My heart thou hast charmèd
Far more than the classic
Outpourer of Massic,
    Horatian barmaid.

In my memory rankles
The turn of thine ankles,
    As thou pourest the nectar ;
Not that I need to
Pay any need to
    Propriety's lecture.

For that angry eyelash down
As thou countest the cash down,
    Tell me too plainly
Of what I'd a notion—
Thou scorn'st my devotion,
    And I sigh for thee vainly !

Thou call'st me " a mere swell,"
Say'st " thou'lt box my ears well "—
    " Thou need'st no protector,
Thyself art sufficient,
Extremely efficient,
    Mad poet ejector ! "

BROWNOROTTO'S DISTEMPER,

And how it worked him.

I.

SHAKE fists, O Harry Owen !
  (Not i' my face, *that's* not the place--
I'm not a fool, I'll not keep cool)
    Egad ! thy missus too ?
    Who's that halloin' ?
    What is all this to-do ?

2.

A pack o' pleasure-goers ?
    Con-found their hunger din !
  Ho ! kick 'em out o' doors,
    Why ever let 'em in ?
O heavens and earth defend us
From this ingens—horrendus—
Confound—infer—tremendous—
Demon—terrif—stupendous—
  And diabolic roar !

3.

Is peace an empty matter?
Or art thou so much fatter
   Thou art from nerves exempt?
Ho, Harry, make a sally
(*Most obvious rime is alley*)
Ere they have time to rally,
Go heave 'em down the valley!

4.

What! treat 'em with contempt,
Say'st thou?   Do th' deed myself!
Bah!   Think'st thou a POET'S hands
Are under thy commands
   To wash thy kitchen delf?
Bah! ha!—— and pshaw.

5.

Ichabod! Ichabod!
It's very odd—very odd—
What! can it be my Roland?
Mine Oliver's own Roland,
   I thought thee under sod
   In Florence wast, or Poland?

6.

Come to a Poet's arms !
    What ! scornest mine embrace ?
Base elf, what counter charms
    Can from thy soul efface
    A Poet's AVATAR ?
" *True counter charms !* " say'st thou,
" *Spirits !* " mutter'st—" *the bar !* "
So like a flash of wonder wrought
The instant answer echoed thought—
    " *Hail, Missus Owen, do*
    Bring glasses quick for two ! "

THE PENALTY OF GREATNESS.

WITH a vile pen, in Harry Owen's book
I write at random, thus:
                    The ivy leaves
That tap the pane are fresher than the bays
About my brows.   I would they had been sere
Or never twinèd there; for I have fled
At the swift heels of steam, to seek afar
The peace a laureate longs for when his liege
Demands a tribute for the laurel crown.
What doth she ask?   A song of Jaune-à-Braune!
From the *Nineteenth Century* have I received
Three hundred pound for less.   Albeit, here goes.

JAUNE-A-BRAUNE.

No little Lilliputian courtier he,
Nor stick in waiting, white nor black nor gold—
A great and granite-headed Norlander,
A Cerberus with all his heads in one,
A lord of lackeys, yet the awe of lords,
A man of title, Jaune-à-Braune, Esquire!
He oped the doors of Pullman carriages,

And no man shut but he—a chieftain eke
Of kilt and philibeg, in whom the clan
Is honourèd, and all the name of Braune
Gain'd by his greatness a full inch or more ;
Yea, all his kin attain'd to affluence
Or bailiffdom at least.

              He, though no more,
Much monumented, church and high hill-cairn
Proclaim his praise, and the insignia
Of a new order, call'd of Jaune-à-Braune,
With motto " *Honi soi.*"

                " A letter for you, sir—
Upon the service of her Majesty ! "
   What meaneth this ? Ah, 'tis that very crown
I placed to usury i' the post-office
Ere yet I left Southampton—the receipt
Come in due course.

            Lo, what is this I see—
HER MAJESTY COMMANDS, and that weird name
Thereafter, *Jaune-à-Braune.*

              O for a lodge
In some vast wilderness or Currie's ship
With Gladstone—*Gladstone !* By the rood !
A great thought strikes along my pen,
And brazens all my cheek. I know the man,
With hearty right good will, he'll turn into
Italian the song that doth begin
About the body of Jaune Braune, that lies

And moulders i' the dust !   He'll do it, 'twixt
The empire and the axe !

                     Alfred the Great,
Thyself applauds thee—this is more
Than all poetic fame, though maybe not
Quite so remunerative.   Haste, then, to catch
The London mail—not the quaint four-in-hand
That once I saw, three piebalds and a roan ;
But wheezy engine dragging snuff-boxes.
Gladstone, I greet thee !

                   I'll not miss that train !

THE MAN WHO LAUGHED NO MORE.

A Neo-archaic Tale.

ARGUMENT.

A certain poet, who also made much goodly house-gear, as he
passed by the way was met by a company of dolorous men. They
beseech him to have himself ware of a hoary man who should meet
him, and entice him to climb with him certain very high hills that
were in that country.

But he made naught of their entreaties and would not be dis-
suaded, and so it happed that he learned their secret to his own
cost and discomfiture soon thereafter.

> Now when the hottest of the season came,
> A poet of an ancient Cymric name
> Did pass this way and in this house abode.
> But as he pondered on the wierdsome road
> Of loss and gain and carven legs of chairs,
> Of culture and of cunning wall-papèrs,
> Of La Commune, with face all grimy-grey,
> Sudden a band of strangers stopp'd his way.
> Batter'd and sad, and ever wearily,
> They eyed his bag to see what there might be.
>
> "We bin no cut-purse knaves, have thou no fear,
> But for thy warning are we gathered here.

M

Oh, go not thither, it will work thee woe,
For what hath thus befallen us, we know.
By the wayside doth lurk a grey-beard man,
To vex thee ere the threshold thou hast wan,
And if his counsel thou do not disdain,
Surely and soothly he will be thy bane!"
　　Then vanish'd they, like witches anciently
That witch'd upon the borders of the sea.
Now right wrong-headed was this foolish wight,
Nor feared he wizardry in broad daylight;
Yet when an olden reverend man he met,
He reck'd not of their idle words, but let
The old man lead him whithersome he would.

　　So hillward went he, saying it was good
That man should be a-merry, therefore he
Would cheer his doleful heart right wondrously,
With antique stories, quaint and strange and true,
And ancient quips the wise mound-builders knew.
So all that day, he murmured ceaselessly,
And the wind fell upon the Anglian Sea,
And still the stream flow'd on. The new sun rose
Upon a man grown grey with many woes.
　　Then knew he all the wisdom of the men,
And all their secret had he in his ken.
　　After these days, he wandered to this inn,
A broken man, with cheeks grown wondrous thin.
Yea, I that write these grievous things am he
Who goes to join that grey-beard company.

LILITH.

SONNET CI.

To the Earthly Paradise Maker.

How far away from here is Willow-wood?
  How long since Adam's garden wanted Eve,
  And Lilith queen'd it—subtle to deceive—
Cunning to snatch the auriole from Good?

Yea, hers and his dwelt deep in Willow-wood,
  While Lilith wrought her vengeance to achieve—
  In barge of Willow-wood the land they leave,
And on these Cymric hills escape the flood.

Ah, wellaway! among that ancient race
  Sitteth the Master, pale and marvelling,
And maidens, wondrous-throated, watch his face,
  Who scarcely breathe what time he saith this thing,

"O thou my friend, that Jason's quest didst sing,
If Lilith's kin thou art, Heaven grant thee grace!"

THE VISION OF THE MAN ORM.

PREFACE.

I am a mortal, and my surname Orm,
And when I name the name of man, I mean
Myself, the singer of the mystic glamour.
I am THE CELT—remember that, mine host,
In charging for my daily provender,
Lest I rede thee the doom I visionëd
E'en for the man accurst !
I am the Personal in Poetry,
In me the blood of all the races blend—
A prophet, with the spirit of the times ;
A man of many moods, in which I scorn
The full assembly of the gods—Brahma,
Osiris, Apis, and Beëlzebub,
Balder and Brigham Young, Allah and Thor !
So friends, avoid me when the fury teareth,
And quickly seek the pavement opposite.

The Poem.

I am old, methought,
   As the world's day closes,
A people anger-wrought
Far and near have sought
   Me, the Celtic Moses.

For I must admit
   That my Highland people,
Men of little wit,
Might in frantic fit
   Swing me from the steeple.

[This from the mystic mad poetic brain,
To show its mastery of the bounding rime.]

Epilogue to Poem.

How shall I liberate mine Ancient Clan,
Clamp'd in the iron fetters of their creeds,
Who care for Sabbath desecration,
And regulating traffic on that day,
More than the poet's realistic vague !
   Who doubt the singer's sprouting pinions—
Yea, hint at clovën foot and forkëd tail
Under the boot and coat immaculate.
   Ah well ! I·pardon them ; they will not read
The hundrëd prefaces and epilogues
In which I body forth my THEORY,

Nor buy my novels; when they name my plays
They spit like blank phantasmic toads—
And shriek ! !

Envoi to Epilogue.

And so in lieu of mintëd Mammon meanness
I offer to my brothër Cymric Celt
These awful visions of the man Buchanan.

FROM PHILIP DRUNK TO PHILIP SOBER.

BY PHILIP I.

I.

From the depth and the dark of the dim city closes,
    And the publishing houses that sprinkle the Strand,
I have come to a land where a poet composes,
    And in infinite series his volumes expand.
From Faustine and Felise, and from Fragioletto,
    From the vine-wreath'd cup in the banqueting hall,
Though I promised to Chatto to write a libretto,
    Grey spirit of Snowdon, I come at thy call.

TRANSLATION BY PHILIP II.

Feeling seedy,
    Looking queer,
    Rather needy,
    Drifted here.

II.

Lo, I stand at thy base, 'mid the mists that environ,
    While shadows cerulean are gambolling round ;
I'm not very clear, for the earth seems of iron,
    As it rises aloft and caresses my crown.
Like a helmless bark whose ways are uncertain,
    Whose captain lists for a God's glad word ;
I wrap me around in the red window curtain,
    And hearken the voice of a songless bird.

TRANSLATION.

Good Scots' whiskey
Makes one see
Demons frisky,
Frequently.

III.

In the dimness and depth of Night's tremulous shadow,
    I gaze on a sight that the sun hath not seen,
The far drifted blooms of the star-sown meadow,
    And their glamorous grey efflorescence of sheen.
They shine on the slopes like Spanish flies glimmering,
    That blister the throat of my Lady of Pain,
Or poultice of herbs of the Orient simmering
    That clings to it softly and heals it again.

TRANSLATION.

Standing nightly
On the road,
Mellow slightly,
Things look odd.

IV.

Like a fiery eye in the gloom set a-smoulder,
   Overfrown'd by the brow of the imminent eaves,
The light of the inn makes the darkness seem colder,
   And enhances the glamour my poet-heart weaves.
But a voice from the midst of the Pleiades seven,
   Or mayhap from the Inn 'twas Ap Owen that cried,
" You had better be quick, for we shut at eleven,
   Unless you're determin'd to slumber outside ! "

TRANSLATION.

Poem sprouteth
In my head ;
Landlord shouteth,
" Come to bed !"

END OF " HARRY OWEN'S BOOK."

1883.

LOVE AND NATURE.

———✦◇✦———

GREETING.

(WRITTEN ON GOATFELL, ARRAN, EARLY MORNING.)

In morning's clear dispersèd light thy peak
  Draws me aloft, O Mountain of the Wind;
    The girdling pasture-lands I leave behind,
'Twixt Cyclopean walls my way I seek,

The strength of strongest hills, albeit weak
  The elemental forces to withstand.
    Within the mighty hollow of thy hand
Thou holdest me; awe keepeth my soul meek.

And yet my heart is at thy seaward base—
  One house is more than all thy majesty,
    One maiden more than suns that ever were

In morning lands or on thy mountain ways—
  Yearneth my heart as yearneth for the sea
    The tumbling waters of thy White Water.

1883.

LOVE AND NATURE.

I.

On this smooth steep of grey and parchèd grass
  Stretch'd out I lie, and all the Lothian plain,
Barrier'd by hills, beneath mine eye doth pass,
  Even from our citadel to where the rain

Swoops from the cloud on the low Lammermoors—
  But what boots all this wealth of summer sweets,
This width of plough-land, Pentland's large contours,
  When a dull inward sense of loss defeats

The beauty and the wisdom, and all meaning steals
  From what a week agone was laden with it ?
    Ah, sweet ! those eyes of thine are more to me

Than all the Gilead-balm that nature deals ;
  Better by thy sweet side an hour to sit
    Than all the beauty of the world to see !

And thou ?—what dost *thou* do ?   Sitt'st thou apart
   Under the hawthorn tree ? or here and there dost go,
Ordering all things with daintiest art ?
   But whatsoe'er she doth, right well I know

My love hath thought for me, forgetteth not
   Aught that hath happ'd between us twain.
Her eyes may 'rest on southern garden plot,
   Yet in them is a yearning and a pain ;

And she had liefer see a sterner land,
   And basalt-bastion'd hills and greyer fields,
      Than bide alone so long and hide her heart.

Love, true and tender, reach me here thine hand ;
   Think, sweet, how much of hope the Future yields,
      When Fate shall not for always say " Apart ! "

1883.

MEMORY AND HOPE.

Out of the clinging valley mists I stray
  Into the summer midnight clear and still,
And which the brighter is no man may say—
  Whether the gold beyond the western hill

Where late the sun went down, or the faint tinge
  Of lucent green, like sea wave's inner curve   .
Just ere it breaks, that gleams behind the fringe
  Of eastern coast. So which doth most preserve

My wistful soul in hope and steadfastness
  I know not—all that golden-memoried past
    So sudden wonderful, when new life ran

First in my veins ; or that clear hope, no less
  Orient within me, for whose sake I cast
    All meaner ends into these ground mists wan.

PRESENCE IN ABSENCE.

THE mists lie in the hollows of the hills,
   In wreaths festoon the ridges; but the heights
   Are clear and bare—a few blurred lights
Gleam yellow from below; but starlight fills

The lucid vault of night; the air is sweet,
   And the far Pentland range is not less clear
   Though darker than by day—distinct and near
The crags arise of Arthur's royal seat—

But whose dear hand is this that guideth me?
   What subtle dainty pressure thrilleth all
     My lonely life?   Who leads me by the way

That overclimbs the mist, and makes me see
   Where Purity abides, whate'er befall
     My mist-environ'd life by night or day.

LOVE'S FINAL CAUSE.

WHAT is it that I love?   The tender glow,
  And faint half-shadows on thy golden hair?
  Thine eyes as clear as summer morning air?
Yea, these—yet not for these alone I love thee so.

Is it that rest and solace go with thee?
  That all my happinesses in thee dwell?
  Is it for these I love thee passing well?
Yea, dearest—but the springs yet deeper flow—

Ask some vext trader far on Indian seas
  Why he runs races with the hurricanes,
    Or floating weed, tide-driven out from land,

Why it returns not shoreward with the breeze.
  Love hath no law—it comes and it remains;
    Yea, stays for ever, daring all command.

TO THE AUTHOR OF "OLRIG GRANGE."

My friend, to thee from out the silent ranks
Of those thou knowest not, who yet give thanks

For all they owe thy mellow thoughtfulness,
I send a brother's greeting— for no less

We in the turmoil love thy fearless truth,
And ever youthful sympathy with youth,

Than they who daily know thy kindly voice,
And quiet shepherding 'mid city noise.

No Jack o'-Lantern glimmer lights thy book,
No moth burns here the fringes of her wing,

Nor gleams thy torch o'er any carnival,
But broad sunshine, which foul things may not brook,

Yet men may work by, till the hours do bring,
After the noon, the mists of evenfall.

1881.

THE LADY BEATRICE.

My love is like that lady Beatrice
   Who held great Dante's heart, whose beauty grew
   So marvellous to his thought, that he would do
All things to give his wistful longing ease—

To touch her hand would overpass the seas,
   To do her will would into exile go,
   Or in the dust a city's headship throw,
If so his well-belovèd lady please.

So loved art thou, Queen Soul, that sitt'st above
   These turmoils in the whirling straits of life,
Reaching a steady hand to stay thy love,
   Vext with the waters, weary of the strife—

Whose feeblest songs of thee impart him peace
Like Dante's when he sang of Beatrice.

1883.

N

THE FOOTPRINTS OF THE GOTH.

RHIADYR-Y-WENNOL, CAERNARVONSHIRE.

THE Vandal and the Visigoth come here,
  The trampler under foot, and he whose eyes,
  Unblest, behold not where the glory lies ;
The wallower in mire, whose sidelong leer

Degrades the wholesome earth—these all come near
  To gaze upon the wonder of the hills,
  And drink the limpid clearness of the rills.
Yet each returns to what he holds most dear,

To change the script and grind the mammon mills
  Unpurified ; for what men hither bring,
    That take they hence, and Nature doth appear

One that doth spend herself for sodden wills,
  That pearls of price before the swine doth fling,
    And from the shrine casts out the sacred gear

188 .

FOR MY MOTHER.

HARD is it, O my friends, to gather up
   A whole life's goodness into narrow space—
   A life made Heaven-meet by patient grace,
And handling oft the sacramental cup

Of sorrow, drinking all the bitter drains.
   Her life she kept most sacred from the world ;
   Though Martha-wise, much cumber'd and imperill'd
With service, Mary-like she brought her pains,

And laid them and herself low at the feet,
   The travel-weary, deep-scarr'd feet, of Him
   The incarnate Good, who oft in Galilee

Had borne Himself the burden and the heat—
   Ah ! couldst thou hear, thy tender eyes were dim
   With humble tears to think this meant for thee !

1880.

CARPE DIEM.

I saw two lovers on a day of days,
   A day of winds spray-tossing, and the swift
   Glad interchange of shine and shade, the drift
Of Atlantean clouds, the heavens that raise

. On their white shoulders ; round them the mid-noon
   Pulsed warmly with the sense of summer air,
   A far thing seem'd the weight of winter care,
And the " Asunder," coming all too soon.

Then my sad heart did say, " Lo, this is well ;
   Take they their fill of love and joy to-day,
    To-morrow, and the next day ; ere the shears

Of Atropos divide them, do thou tell
   Those twain their hearts to strengthen while they may,
    And so stand firm through all the lonely years.

1884.

THE LIFTING OF THE VEIL.

In the still dewy morn of Western Isles,
 Up some lone loch far in the Hebrides,
 I hear among the heath the honey bees,
And the long level lake in sunshine smiles :

I round the cliff, a roaring in mine ears—
 For miles and miles the grey Atlantic booms,
 As down the coast the breaker surging comes
Whitecrested, like a rush of mountaineers.

So too, a youth, whose feet in quiet ways
 Have gone through all his years, exploring bold
  By speculation's vast and trackless sea,

Finds realms undreamt of in his careless days
 Flash on his sight—at noon the copestone rolled
  From whited sepulchres' hypocrisy.

1877.

THE WEB OF LIFE.

I.

In the cool precinct of a quiet room,
  Lit by the glory of the northern eves,
  Her web of life a maiden sits and weaves—
Gold web of pleasure, purple fringe of gloom.

Some after-rose of the late sunset's bloom
  Cleaves to her cheek and robing virginal,
  And softly round about her feet doth fall
The cloth of gold she weaveth on her loom,

As through and through the steadfast weft of love
  She drives the shining thread of memories—
Here fashioning a waste of waves—above,
  Two hands that clasp a golden Fleur-de-lis ;
And higher, ONE, whose emblem is the dove,
  Broodeth for always over the grey seas.

II.

Far sever'd from the first by measured miles,
　　Another web is woven and other hands
　　Ply the swift shuttle, guide the shining strands
To form that strange compound of tears and smiles,

Glad hearted laughter, dear delicious wiles
　　That make the mantle of Love's hidden form,
　　And interwoven arms more close and warm
Because the earth is chilly and the aisles

Of Life's high temple, builded all of stone,
　　Too unresponsive to humanity
For man or maid to dwell in all alone.
　　So grows on each the pattern we shall see
One day by Love's hands round our shoulders drawn—
　　A wedding garment fit for thee and me.

　1884.

SPRING YEARNING.

TO R. W.

NEW lands, strange faces, all the summer days
　My weary feet **have trod,** mine eyes have seen ;
　Among the snows all winter have **I** been,
Rare Alpine air, **and white** untrodden ways.

From the great Valais mountain peaks my **gaze**
　Hath seen the cross on Monte **Viso** plain,
　Seen blue Maggiore grey with driving rain,
And white cathedral spires like flames of **praise.**

Yet now the spring **is** here, who doth **not** sigh
　For showery **morns,** and grey skies **sudden** bright,
　And a dear **land** a-dream with shifting **light** !
Or in what clear-skied realm doth ever lie,

Such glory as of gorse **on Scottish braes,**
Or the white hawthorn **of these English Mays?**

1885.

HOPE DEFERRED.

BARE is the waste sea-margin in the dawn,
   Barren the baffled ebbing of the tide,
   Grey tracks of shingle, miles on either side ;
Here is no trace of any work of man,

Above and underfoot God's perfect plan,
   Unbounded, vast, and fill'd with loneliness—
   Swift race of breakers, ranks of cloud that press
Hard in the breeze's wake, whose rare draught ran

Clear through my heart and cool'd its burning thirst.
   Here o'er and o'er I conn'd this barren lore :
   " *Than Hope deferr'd, better Hope lost at first.*"
   Until upon the barren salt sea-shore,

Forsaken by the ebb's forlorn regress,
I wept for love and utter loneliness.

1884.

ANCHORA FIDEI.

WHEN from the depths of an unclouded sky
  The thunderbolt doth fall, or earthquake waves
  Threaten the sleeping city, he who saves
His sacredest possession, doth not cry

With bootless wailing, or inactive lie
  Waiting the crash of doom.   Nay, he doth face
  The terror of great darkness, firmly brace
His feet against some bar of faith, or try

Which bands are iron, which of twisted straw ;
  And most rejoic'd is he, who then hath found
    The one sure band that may not broken be,

That in the tempest Faith doth closer draw
  Until her arms engird his body round,
    And bring his soul in safety through the sea.

1883.

LOVE IN A WORLD OF SNOW.

On either side the great and still ice sea
  Are compassing snow mountains near and far ;
  While dominant Schreckhorn and Finsteraar
Hold their grim peaks aloft defiantly.

Blind with excess of light and glory, we,
  Above whose heads in hottest mid-day glare
  The Schreckhorn and his sons arise in air,
Sink in the weary snowfields to the knee ;

Then, resting after peril pass'd in haste,
  I saw, from our rock-shelter'd vantage ledge,
  In the white fervent heat sole shadowy spot,

Familiar eyes that smiled amid the waste—
  Lo ! in the sparse snow at the glacier edge,
  The small blue flower we call Forget-me-not !

1884.

PRO FANO.

HAIL, World-adored ! to thee three times all hail !
  We at thy mighty shrine, profane, obscure,
  With clenchèd hands beat at thy cruel door.
O hear, awake, and let us in, O Baal !

Low at thy brazen gates ourselves we fling—
  Hear us, ev'n us, thy bondmen firm and sure,
  Our thoughts, our souls, our very God abjure !
Art thou asleep, or dead, or journeying?

Hear us, O Ashtoreth, O Baal, that we
  In mystic mazes may a moment gleam,
May touch and twine with hot hearts pulsing free
  Among thy groves by the Orontes stream.

Open and make us, ere our sick hearts fail,
Hewers of wood within thy courts, O Baal !

December, 1885.

A CREED FOR MEN—OR DEVILS?

" BEHOLD the Final Truth of cosmic things !
   All is unreal, all the shifting play
   Of lights that gild a horror of decay—
A gold dome charnelling worm-eaten kings.

No truth in God—or is there any God?
   The *universe,* dead matter, working by
   Some hidden yeast of inward energy ;
Mind, but mere brain-cell, good to feed the sod ;

No whence or whither, just a Nothing thrown
   In th' empty space betwixt two Nothingnesses.
     But live—live on, O men ; be loath to end

This vegetable life ! You'll not be mown
   This sickle sweep ; so kiss the heel that presses,
     And bless your gods for these good gifts they send ! "

1882.

A VOICE CRYING.

WHO calls it harm to play this pleasant game,
Or Folly's ball to toss from hand to hand?
　　And, while the feet are light, why should one stand
Out in the corridor among the lame?

Nay, entering rather, hearken the acclaim
That is our welcome to the lightsome band,
　　Who whirl so swiftly through Queen Pleasure's land,
Whom Thought may not annoy, nor Conscience blame.

Shut out the stars and the fair universe—
　　Shut out the silent spaces of the wood;
Let not that wild wail from the darkness pierce

　　The graceful lightness of our airy mood—
"*Ah, had I known, when just as gay was I,*
That in the waste, untended, I should lie!"

1884.

TIME'S NEMESIS.

Ho, let the viol's pleasing swifter grow—
    Let Music's madness fascinate the will,
    And all Youth's pulses with the ardour thrill !
Hast thou, Old Time, e'er seen so brave a show?

Did not the dotard smile as he said "*No ?*"
    Pshaw ! hang the grey-beard—let him prate his fill ;
    Men are but dolts who talk of Good and Ill.
These grapes of ours are wondrous sour, I trow !

They sneer because we joy in other things,
    And think they know THE GOOD.   I tell the fools
We have the pleasure—WE ! *Our* master flings
    Full-measured bliss to all the folk he rules,

Nor asks he aught for quit-rent, fee, or tithe—
Ho, Bald-head, wherefore sharpenest thy scythe ?

  1884.

TO JOHN GREENLEAF WHITTIER,
THE FRIEND—MY FRIEND.

NORTH of the North Cape I remember thee,
  Brave Quaker poet of the New World North!
  To thee, my friend, in silence goeth forth
Into the keen air of this Arctic sea,

Greeting and filial reverence heartily.
  As when in shade of gardens summer-leaved
  Thy first grave benediction I received,
Or when in towerèd town more dear to me

Thou bad'st me God-speed in the young man's race,
  I am thy liegeman still, and humbly kneel
Between thy scarrèd hands to lay my face—
  Desiring most thy pure heart·fire to steal,
A double portion of thy spirit's grace,
  And ardour for an equal Commonweal.

1885.

MARIE.

(FROM ALFRED DE MUSSET'S " POÉSIES NOUVELLES.")

I.

As from spring buds in woodlands
  Break mystical smiles,
At the breathing of warm airs
  From westerly isles ;

II.

As their stems, fresh and tender,
  Shake with joy and desire,
From their roots in earth's bosom
  To their cups full of fire ;

III.

So soareth my love's song
  As upward it goes
When she stirreth to music
  A mouth like a rose

O

IV.

And her lover stands listening
    How thrillingly true,
Rings the voice that is hovering
    Far up in the blue.

1885.

BIRTHDAY BLESSING.

Be brave and true to God alone,
    And without fear
Do thou rejoice to enter on
    Another year.

Each spring the trees are fresh and green;
    The springing flowers
In fair fresh dress each year are seen
    In thy still bowers.

So keep thy maiden heart as bright;
    Each year renew
Thy soul's apparel of delight
    In all things true;

And long ere winter's twilight falls
    With chill and damp,
And at the door the Bridegroom calls,
    Trim thou thy lamp.

1885.

LISA OF THE HILL.

INTO the hotter sun
  Out of the old stone wall,
Lithe lizards flash and run
  And slow soft blind-worms crawl.

Lisa among the leaves,
  Under her hat's brown brim,
A web of fancy weaves,
  What she shall say to him—

How she shall bid him go
  To Netta of the Mill,
And no more trouble know
  Through Lisa of the Hill.

All in the cloudless glow
  Lisa doth dress the vines ;
Yet Lisa's self doth go
  Among the shady pines.

Along their forest tracks
  Her heart flits on the wing,
Round where she hears the axe
  Of woodman Petro ring—

Petro, whose sunburnt face
  And sunny Lombard curls,
Whose open forest ways,
  Are lov'd of Lombard girls.

Boldly will Lisa say
  To Petro words severe ;
Petro shall turn away,
  In wondering and in fear.

But, swiftly driven apart,
  Just then the leaves divide,
And Lisa with a start
  Turneth her head aside.

And lo, two hands are laid
  Upon her shoulders so,
That 'neath the vine-leaves' shade
  Hotly her cheek doth glow :

And though a stalwart arm
 Somehow is round her waist,
Lisa takes no alarm,
 Nor shows a sign of haste.

She goes an inch more near,
 And, speaking somewhat low,
She saith her words severe
 And biddeth him to go.

But he who comes to stay
 Turns not so quick again,
So all the summer day
 Netta may watch in vain.

And Petro needs not fear ;
 For, turning up her head,
Something much less severe
 Her tell-tale eyes have said ;

When he, through broad green leaves
 Moves as to go away,
He sees a face that grieves,
 Two lips that murmur "Stay !"

Then dainty finger-tips
 Make for his eyes a hood,
The while her daintier lips
 Behave as red lips should.

Ah, Netta of the Mill,
 Long mayst thou lonely brood,
With Lisa of the Hill
 Stays Petro of the Wood.

1885.

ASCRIPTION

*With Aldrich's " Queen of Sheba" and with
" Dulce Cor."*

U<small>NTO</small> another Ruth,
  Not woo'd 'neath Savoy pine,
Fair in her queenly youth,
  Not Sheba's queen, but mine.

1886.

PRINTED BY WILLIAM CLOWES AND SONS, LIMITED,
LONDON AND BECCLES.